The legacy of a kidnapp
sets Dane Maddock and ᴅᴏᴜᴇꜱ ᴅᴏᴜᴇʙᴜᴜᴀᴋᴇ ᴏᴜ ᴀ ᴄᴏᴜᴜꜱᴜᴏᴜ
course with a deadly organization that will stop at
nothing to claim the greatest treasure in history. But
more than riches are at stake. Enemies old and new and
even old friends stand in Maddock's way in a struggle to
control the mysterious power unlocked by the
SOLOMON KEY.

PRAISE FOR DAVID WOOD
AND THE DANE MADDOCK ADVENTURES

"David Wood has done it again. Within seconds of
opening the book, I was hooked. Intrigue,
suspense,monsters, and treasure hunters. What more
could you want? David's knocked it out of the park with
this one!" -Nick Thacker, author of *The Enigma Strain*

"A page-turning yarn blending high action, Biblical
speculation, ancient secrets, and nasty creatures. Indiana
Jones better watch his back!" Jeremy Robinson, author
of *SecondWorld*

"Dane and Bones.... Together they're unstoppable. Rip
roaring action from start to finish. Wit and humor
throughout. Just one question - how soon until the next
one? Because I can't wait." Graham Brown, author of
Shadows of the Midnight Sun

"What an adventure! A great read that provides lots of
action, and thoughtful insight as well, into strange
realms that are sometimes best left unexplored." Paul
Kemprecos, author of *Cool Blue Tomb* and *the NUMA
Files*

SOLOMON
KEY

A DANE MADDOCK ADVENTURE

DAVID WOOD

Solomon Key, A Dane Maddock Adventure

Published by Adrenaline Press
www.adrenaline.press
Adrenaline Press is an imprint of Gryphonwood
Press
www.gryphonwoodpress.com

Cover by Kent Holloway Book Cover Design

This book is a work of fiction. All events, locations, and characters depicted are products of the author's imagination or are used fictitiously.

ISBN-10: 1-940095-77-8
ISBN-13: 978-1-940095-77-6

BOOKS BY DAVID WOOD

THE DANE MADDOCK ADVENTURES
Dourado
Cibola
Quest
Icefall
Buccaneer
Atlantis
Ark
Xibalba
Loch
Solomon Key

DANE AND BONES ORIGINS
Freedom
Hell Ship
Splashdown
Dead Ice
Liberty
Electra
Amber
Justice
Treasure of the Dead

JADE IHARA ADVENTURES (WITH SEAN ELLIS)
Oracle
Changeling
Exile

BONES BONEBRAKE ADVENTURES
Primitive
The Book of Bones

JAKE CROWLEY ADVENTURES (WITH ALAN BAXTER)
Blood Codex
Anubis Key

BROCK STONE ADVENTURES
Arena of Souls
Track of the Beast (forthcoming)

MYRMIDON FILES (WITH SEAN ELLIS)
Destiny
Mystic

STAND-ALONE NOVELS
Into the Woods (with David S. Wood)
The Zombie-Driven Life
You Suck
Callsign: Queen (with Jeremy Robinson)
Dark Rite (with Alan Baxter)
Primordial (with Alan Baxter)

DAVID WOOD WRITING AS DAVID DEBORD

THE ABSENT GODS TRILOGY
The Silver Serpent
Keeper of the Mists
The Gates of Iron

The Impostor Prince (with Ryan A. Span)
Neptune's Key

PROLOGUE
Off the coast of Jamaica

Peter Archer, or Red Pete as he was known to his crewmates, crept silently across the deck of the *Blue Crane*, which lay at anchor in sight of Port Royal. It was a moonless night, and the crew lay in drunken slumber after a night in port. Even the captain had imbibed to excess. This might be Pete's only chance.

He crept belowdecks, making his way down to the hold where *Blue Crane's* human cargo was bound. His heart raced. Could he really do this? Why was he risking his life for someone he barely knew?

"He's your friend," he whispered to himself. "Maybe your only friend."

He smelled the cargo hold long before he reached it. The foul odor of humans kept at close quarters for a prolonged period. The foul stench of sweat mingled with the stink of feces, urine, and stale air. He retched as he unlocked the hold and clambered down into the midst of the Africans who would soon be sold at auction.

Caesar was awake. His dark skin rendered him nigh invisible down here in the blackness of the hold. He sensed, rather than saw, Pete.

"What are you doing?" he hissed. His English was improving rapidly, but his accent remained heavy.

"Don't talk."

Pete unlocked the chains that bound Caesar's wrists and ankles, and helped the big man to stand.

"Follow me." He led Caesar out of the hold and up to the next deck.

"We're getting out of here," he said softly. "Everyone's drunk. Even the captain. We'll steal a boat and lose ourselves in Port Royal."

"What will we do?"

Pete shrugged. "I don't know. Sign on to a pirate's crew, maybe? They won't care who we are or where we're from."

Caesar nodded.

"I must have my ring."

"Your what?

"My ring. The one the captain took from me. I must have it back."

Pete remembered the ring. It was very old. Not worth anything, the captain had said, yet he had worn it ever since taking it from the captured African warrior.

"The captain has it."

"Show me the way," Caesar said.

Pete ran a hand through his stringy red hair. What was Caesar thinking? "Are you mad? If he wakes, we're both of us done for."

Caesar grabbed him by the arm. *Damn, the man was strong.* "He will not wake. Show me."

Trembling with fear, Pete guided Caesar to the captain's cabin and stood watch, determined to leap overboard if anyone discovered him. After what felt like an eternity, Caesar returned. He wore his ring and a satisfied smile.

"He will not wake again. Let us go."

Every little noise sounded like a gunshot to Pete. The soft pad of their feet on the deck, every breath. He was certain his heart must sound like a snare drum to everyone on board.

Finally, blessedly, they found themselves in the dinghy rowing for port. Caesar had never rowed before, but he caught on quickly, driving them through the water with powerful strokes Pete could never hope to match.

Just as he was beginning to relax, the moon broke through the clouds, and he saw movement on board *Blue Crane.*

"There they are!" a voice called.

A shot rang out, the slug splashing in the water just feet from their boat.

Caesar stopped rowing.

"What in the Seven Hells are you doing? They're shooting at us!"

Caesar stared at the ship, seemingly unaware of Pete's presence. He touched the ring on his hand and whispered something.

Pete jerked upright as a cloud of mist surrounded them. Shouts from the ship told him the crew members were as confused as he.

The wind began to rise, whipping the calm waters into a frenzy of whitecaps. Pete grabbed hold of the gunwale and began to pray.

A roar filled his ears, the shouts of the crew turning to screams. He heard the sound of ripping canvas, the snap of broken boards.

And then silence.

He opened his eyes to see calm waters. No sign of *Blue Crane.* He turned to Caesar, unable to speak.

"Now," Caesar said, returning to the oars, "we will go be pirates."

CHAPTER 1
Caesar's Spring, Florida

The sun beat down on his bare shoulders as Dane Maddock broke through the tree line and stepped to the edge of the water. The spring-fed sinkhole was impossibly blue, its steep sides running straight down into the dark depths. He stood there, staring down, wondering what secrets it might hide. He would soon find out.

"Now this is my idea of a dive site." Bones Bonebrake, Maddock's partner and former colleague in the Navy SEALs, looked around, nodding approvingly.

"Bones, you are not even looking at the spring."

"You look at what interests you; I'll pay attention to what I'm interested in." The powerfully built, six and a half foot tall Cherokee grinned as his eyes swept the shore, taking in the many bikini-clad young women. "Matter of fact, I think we should skip the dive altogether. There's plenty of treasure up here."

"You are all class, Bones," Maddock said.

"And you've been even more curmudgeonly than usual since you broke up with my sister." Bones held up a big hand, forestalling Maddock's retort. "Look, I get it. The two of you broke up, the chick you were hot for turned out to be a bad guy. That would piss me off, too. But all the more reason to avail yourself of the local hospitality."

"That's not exactly how it happened," Maddock said. But, Bones was essentially correct. He and his fiancée, make that ex-fiancée, Angel Bonebrake, had agreed to take some time off from their relationship. The breakup had happened *after* Isla Mulheron had abandoned them in Scotland. He supposed he was splitting hairs with that distinction.

Bones was paying him no mind. He was grinning at a pair of brunettes clad in Confederate flag bikinis. The girls were smiling back, clearly enjoying the attention.

"Did you say something?" he asked.

"I thought you didn't like rednecks," Maddock said, casting a meaningful glance at the women's attire.

"Usually I don't, but I suppose I could make an exception." He turned and arched an eyebrow. "Live a little, Maddock. Who knows? One of them might be into short little blond dudes."

Maddock smirked. Sturdily built and just a hair over six feet tall, he was hardly short or little, but most people looked small when standing alongside Bones. "Don't be so cocky. You know how cold these spring-fed pools are. Those girls might not be so interested in you once you come back out of the water, Mr. Shrinkage."

"You know, that's not cool. Besides, that was a long time ago."

"But it did happen. I've got witnesses."

"Screw you, Maddock. Let's dive."

Chuckling, Maddock strapped on his dive gear and checked his equipment while Bones did the same. He had been looking forward to this dive ever since hearing about Caesar's Spring. Located in the Florida Panhandle, the spring had been kept a secret by the owners of the land upon which it was located, and had only recently been open to the public. To Maddock's knowledge, no serious divers had investigated it. The odds of anything of value being found there were slim, but that was not at the top of his list. For him, it was the chance to be the first to explore the underwater passages that fed the spring.

"Why do you think they call it Caesar's Spring?" Maddock said aloud, not really asking.

"Beats me," Bones said. "The only Caesar I'm really interested in is Caesar's Palace."

"Philistine."

"You say that like it's a bad thing." Bones moved to the edge of the water and jumped in feet first. Seconds later, his head broke the surface. "Holy freaking crap. How cold is this water?" he sputtered.

"Sixty-eight degrees year-round." Maddock couldn't

help but laugh. "What did you expect from a pool fed by spring water? It's not like it's the first one we've dived."

"I try to block those out of my mind as quickly as possible. Now, get your ass in here. This was your idea, after all."

Maddock plunged into the water. Even in his diving suit, it was a shock to his system. No matter how many times he did it, diving in frigid water was not something one grew accustomed to.

The daylight fled as they descended through the crystalline waters until they reached the bottom. Here, the world was blanketed in shadow, like the last hours of dusk. He flipped on his headlamp, swam to the center of the pool, and began moving in a slow circle, gradually working his way outward. Bones swam alongside him. Maddock knew his friend would rather swim to and fro without a plan, simply taking it all in. Maddock preferred a methodical approach, not wanting to miss anything.

Looking down, Maddock could see the detritus-choked bottom, all covered in a layer of silt. It was possible, he supposed, that something of value lay beneath the ground here. They wouldn't know without a metal detector, and perhaps not even then. Considering the site's remote location, they would likely only find bits of rubbish and not much else. He and Bones were treasure hunters by trade. They'd enjoyed a few big scores lately, and weren't interested in scavenging for scraps. Anyway, he wasn't here to work—he was here to relax and forget his troubles.

The spring was a good twenty meters in diameter, but they quickly worked their way out to the edge. Down here the lack of sunlight and the frigid waters kept the vegetation to a minimum. It was all silt and rocks.

It wasn't long before they found what they were looking for–an underwater passageway leading back into the darkness. It was more than large enough for the two of them to swim abreast. Bones turned to him and gave the thumbs-up.

Maddock nodded. This was both the most exciting and most dangerous part of freshwater diving. It was easy to get lost in passageways like these. They often branched off in many directions, and if one was not careful, a diver kicking too hard could stir up a cloud of silt, blinding them. Many divers had lost their lives in Florida's freshwater springs. In fact, in most places, the authorities had posted harsh warnings to that effect. There were no such signs here, at least not yet.

Maddock unhooked his reel line from his belt and secured one end just inside the entrance to the passageway. With this to both help them find their way back and mark their distance, he and Bones swam into the darkness. The going was slow, but they managed to make their way along without disturbing the fine particles that coated the walls. A gentle current worked against them, but it provided little in the way of resistance. Within a few meters they found themselves in utter darkness, their headlamps slicing through the blackness. While many people would've found the confines of this channel constricting, even claustrophobic, Maddock found a certain peace in the utter darkness and complete silence. Furthermore, he and Bones had been in much tighter confines in the past. This was an easy dive so far.

The channel snaked its way back into the bedrock. A few side passages, much too small for a diver to enter, branched off on either side. Maddock was pleased that he saw no signs that anyone had been here before.

He'd always been fascinated with exploration. As a youth, he had devoured books about the great explorers in world history and in his subsequent career he'd had a few opportunities to come to find things that had gone on undiscovered for centuries or more. There was a thrill that came with knowing he was the first person to explore a place, or at least the first in a very long time.

The passageway finally branched off in two directions, and they paused to decide their next move. Maddock looked at Bones who gave a noncommittal wave of his hand as if to say, "Whichever."

Maddock checked his air to make sure they were still in good shape. They could safely go on a little bit longer. But which way?

They were spared the decision when a cloud of silt suddenly poured forth from the passageway to their right. Maddock flashed a confused glance at Bones, not that either could see the other very well with their masks on. Had something collapsed up ahead? He moved up for a closer look, and his answer came in an instant.

A diver, flailing wildly, crashed into him. Maddock had been diving for most of his life and assessed the situation in an instant. The diver had clearly gotten lost and become panicked. Frantic, the diver clawed at Maddock's regulator. He needed to get control of the situation right away.

He seized the diver, a woman based on her physique, pinning her arms to her sides. She struggled and kicked, but could not break free of his strong grip. Meanwhile, Bones forced her regulator into her mouth and held it there, nodding slowly. The woman kicked Maddock hard in the shin with her heel, and he hooked one leg around hers to keep her motionless. At long last, he felt her stop fighting and relax. Soon she was taking slow regular breaths. Hoping it was safe, Maddock released her from his grasp.

The woman pressed her hands together and made a little bob of her head to express her gratitude. Maddock nodded, then pointed to their guide line, and then motioned back down the passageway. She nodded to indicate that she understood.

Bones led the way on the return journey, with Maddock bringing up the rear to collect the rope. With the current at their backs, they made their way quickly out into the sinkhole and back to the surface, Maddock pausing just long enough to unhook their guide line and finish reeling it in.

They broke the surface at the water's edge. The diver clutched the rock ledge, tore off her mask, and hung there, eyes closed, gasping for breath. Maddock and Bones took up positions on either side of her and waited for her to collect herself. Finally, she looked up and managed a weary smile.

She was beautiful, with big eyes, dark brown skin, and high cheekbones. Her hair was shaved almost down to the scalp, which somehow seemed to emphasize her delicate features and athletic build.

"Thank you," she breathed. Maddock thought he heard a touch of East Africa in her voice. Perhaps Ethiopia. "I was in trouble. I can't believe I panicked like that."

"You were lucky we came along," Bones said. "People die down in those springs all the time. You really shouldn't have been diving alone."

"I don't need you to mansplain diving to me, thank you very much." The woman closed her eyes for a moment, her features relaxing. "Forgive me. I'm embarrassed and angry with myself for making such an amateur decision as to go down there alone without guide markers of any sort. I thought I could do it. I was wrong. In any event, I should not take it out on you."

"No sweat," Bones said. "Nobody's at their best after a dive gone wrong." He flashed a smile. "I'm Bones. This is Maddock."

"I'm Nomi," she said. She hesitated, looking from one man to the other. "I hope you don't mind me saying, but the two of you are a mismatched pair. You don't go together at all."

"You mean because I'm good-looking and he's, well, you see what he's working with." Bones inclined his head toward Maddock.

"I think she means because I'm smart and you're a dim bulb," Maddock said.

Nomi laughed. "You know what I mean. Don't misunderstand. You're both handsome; you just don't go together."

"Actually, you're far from the first to notice," Maddock said. "We were in the service together, Navy

SEALs. Been friends ever since."

"Almost brothers-in-law until my sister dumped his ass," Bones added.

Nomi raised her eyebrows. "Single? I'll remember that."

"Hey, I'm single too," Bones said. "And you don't have to worry about me getting all emo about my exes. Hell, I forget about a girl as soon as I..." The look in Nomi's eye cut him off in midsentence.

"So what brings the two of you to Caesar's Spring? Are you the thrill-seeking type that likes dangerous dives?"

"Maybe a little bit. Mostly we just enjoy diving. When we heard about a new place, we couldn't resist being the first to explore the passageways. Of course, we didn't get here first," Maddock said, grinning.

Mischief sparkled in Nomi's eyes. "Sorry to beat you to it. So, what do the two of you do when you aren't diving?"

"Actually, we're pretty much always diving," Bones said. "We're marine archaeologists."

Maddock didn't miss a slight narrowing of Nomi's eyes. "Treasure hunters?" she asked.

"Yep. Pretty good ones too," Bones said. "Tell you what. We're staying at the campground just off the main road. If you want to drop by later, I'll buy you a beer and tell you all about it."

Nomi's smile was forced. "Maybe."

"So," Maddock began, "what brings you to the spring? Are you also a treasure hunter?"

"No," Nomi said quickly. "I just heard about this place and fancied a dive, same as you." She pushed herself up and clambered out of the water. "I really have to go. But thank you again." She stripped off her fins and hurried away.

They watched her go, Bones clearly admiring the way she moved. When she disappeared from sight, he turned to Maddock.

"That was weird. What do you think?"

"I think," Maddock began, "she's hiding something. But what that something is I have no idea."

CHAPTER 2
Glastonbury Tor

Isla Mulheron smoothed her auburn hair and checked her makeup in the mirror before climbing out of the car. It wasn't that she cared what the man she was meeting thought of her appearance, but she thought it best to maintain a professional air about her at all times. Some of these older men treated women, young women in particular, as adorable idiots. She would not tolerate that.

A stocky, gray-haired man waited for her at the foot of Glastonbury Tor. He stood there, gazing off into the distance, puffing away at a Calabash pipe. She'd never seen one of the pipes outside of a Sherlock Holmes film. Smiling, she headed in his direction.

"Mister Osborne? I'm Isla Mulheron." Osborne was a local amateur historian whom she'd tracked down online.

They shook hands, Osborne frowning a little. "You sounded older when we spoke on the phone."

She wasn't quite certain how to respond to that, so she ignored it. "Thank you for meeting me. I'm eager to learn about the history and legends surrounding the tor." That was almost the truth. Extensive research had led her to this place. Now she was hoping to learn something new—nuggets of local history that might have escaped the attention of scholars.

Osborne took another puff of his pipe. The breeze carried a vanilla-scented cloud of blue smoke Isla's way. The aroma brought back bittersweet memories of her father.

"You said you work for that *Scottish Adventure* magazine?"

"That's right."

He scowled, took another puff. "Glastonbury's not in Scotland," he finally said.

God. Was he going to be such a condescending bawbag for their entire meeting? She forced herself to keep smiling. "Our readers travel all over Britain, so a site with such a long and colorful history will be of great interest to them."

Osborne nodded slowly. "Let's get on with it then."

Isla found she didn't need to ask many questions. She merely turned on her recorder and feigned interest as Osborne droned on about the legends surrounding Glastonbury Tor. Located in the English county of Somerset, the tall, conical hill stood conspicuously in the midst of the surrounding flatlands of the Summerland Meadows. Surmounted by St. Michael's Tower, the tor was the most prominent feature in all the surrounding countryside. It had been given many nicknames over the years: Magic Mountain, Faeries' Glass Hill, Spiral Castle, Grail Castle, and Land of the Dead.

"There's been a lot of legends about the tor over the years," Osborne said. "People call it a magic mountain, claim there's some sort of magnetic power point here because of the ley lines or some such, which made it a landing spot for UFOs. Some say there was a castle here that hid the Holy Grail. Others called it the Isle of Avalon, said it marked the entrance to the underworld. There's also older history here. It's an important site to the Celts. Druids even held fertility rituals here."

Isla shifted uncomfortably. A small voice in the back of her mind said the man could see right through her, knew the real reason she was interested in the tor and its history. But that was absurd. She actually was writing a piece for the magazine. Her ulterior motives were known only to a few.

"Has there been any investigation into the more exotic claims?" she asked.

Osborne chuckled. "How do you investigate the absurd? But yes, there's been people out here from time to time. They bring odd-looking equipment that's supposed to measure magnetism and the like. It's all bollocks."

Isla sensed this was the wrong time to ask probing questions. If the man decided she was only interested in conspiracy theories, she'd lose whatever credibility she might have with him.

"One man swore there was once a crystal castle here." Osborne laughed.

Isla's heart leaped at the mention of a crystal castle. Perhaps she was on the right track.

"I understand the Celtic name of the Tor was *Ynys Wydryn*, or *Ynys Gutrin*, meaning 'Isle of Glass.' Perhaps that's where the legend comes from?"

Osborne raised his eyebrows and looked down at her as if seeing her for the first time. Clearly she had risen in his estimation. "That is correct. Come on. I've got lots more to show you."

He guided her to the Chalice Well, a natural spring said to have been in use for more than two thousand years. Surrounded by manicured gardens, the well, also known as Red Spring, was said to possess healing properties. A popular site among Neopagans, the well was strongly associated with the sacred feminine, with the Tor representing the masculine. All around she saw the trappings of both Christian and Pagan symbolism in the design of the gardens, from the well lid carved with interlocking circles bisected by a sword, down to the seven bowls of the vesica piscis, a shape formed by interlocking circles. Here there were layers upon layers of intrigue, enough to keep a conspiracy theorist busy for a lifetime.

"It's iron oxide deposits what gives the water the reddish tint," Osborne said. "Of course, the storytellers say it's thanks to Joseph of Arimathea. Depending on which story you hear, he either put the Holy Grail in here with drops of the blood of Christ in it, or he dropped in some nails from the crucifixion. Either way, it's…"

"Bollocks," Isla finished for him.

Osborne flashed a crooked smile. "There's a clear spring nearby called the White Spring. They've built a waterworks over it, but it's open to visitors."

"I think I'd like to see the tor if that's all right."

Osborne led her along the steep path leading to the top of the tor. As they climbed, he pointed out the many terraces, now overgrown with lush, green grass.

"No one can agree what these are," he said. "Some say it's just for defense of whatever might have been built up at the top. Others think it was once a spiral path that led to the top."

"What do you think?"

Osborne pursed his lips. "It reminds me of the labyrinth in Greek mythology. I know that sounds mad, but there you are."

"I don't think it's mad at all. The spiral maze was an important symbol in ancient cultures, representing the soul's journey from life to death to rebirth. And as you said, this place has long been associated with the Celts."

Osborne stopped in his tracks and turned to look at her. "Sounds like you already know it all."

"Hardly, but you write enough articles about historic sites in Britain, you pick up a few things."

Osborne seemed to find this an acceptable explanation and they resumed their trek, now cloaked in silence.

At the top, they paused to take in the sights. Isla found herself mesmerized by the view. To the north lay the Mendip Hills and nearby the faint outline of the Wells Cathedral. To the west, the island of Steep Holm in the Bristol Channel. The Black Mountains of Wales loomed hazy far to the southwest. And to the east, Cley Hill, a spot famous for UFO sightings.

"You're lucky it's a clear day," Osborne said. "Can't see a thing on a foggy day. Course, some tourists prefer it that way. The 'mists of Avalon' and all that shite."

Next they examined St. Michael's Tower. The roofless structure was all that remained of what was once St. Michael's Church. Isla found it interesting, but it was not what she was looking for.

"This has been wonderful," she said to Osborne. "Exactly what I needed for my article." She wondered how deeply she could probe before the man dismissed her entirely. "Our readers also enjoy the obscure local legends, even the stuff that's 'bollocks' as you called it. Anything like that you can share with me? The stuff that would play with our readers who love a good conspiracy theory or treasure hunt?" She saw Osborne tense a little and hurried on. "I won't attach your name to it. Just share it as a story I picked up."

"That would be for the best, I think." Osborne scratched his chin. "I already mentioned the aliens and all the esoteric stuff. But as far as conspiracies go, there's always been legends that there's all sorts of tunnels running underneath the hill and even to parts of Glastonbury. There actually was at least one tunnel back in the 1960s. Used to have jazz concerts there. The birds I used to meet at those." A faint smile played over his face, his gaze suddenly far away. After a few seconds of reverie, he gave his head a shake. "Anyhow, whatever is supposed to be hidden here, be it the grail or some other artifact, supposedly can be found at the end of one of the secret tunnels."

Isla nodded, trying to hide her eagerness.

"Legend has it, all the tunnels have collapsed except for one."

"Any idea where it would be? According to legend, I mean," she added.

"Common wisdom is, it runs from beneath the Abbey to the tor, which they claim is hollow underneath. Long ago, thirty monks were rumored to have followed the tunnel down to the tor." He paused. "But only three came out again, two insane and one struck dumb. Like I said, bollocks."

"Maybe, but it makes for an entertaining story. The readers will love it."

Osborne let out a huff of breath through his nose, showing exactly what he thought of those readers.

"Our readers also love Arthurian legend," Isla began, choosing her words with care. "Some of those legends surrounding Glastonbury Tor are well known. But I wonder if, and I'm not quite sure how to put it…"

"Just spit it out. That's always the best way."

"Many of our readers would love to believe there's some historical fact behind those legends. Have there been any discoveries to that end here? Anything at all, no matter how seemingly insignificant, that could lend credence to such a far-fetched theory?"

"Venturing into tabloid territory, are you?" Osborne fished out his pipe and began to pack it again.

"Not at all. I'll make it clear in my article that these are merely colorful local legends."

Osborne considered this for the length of time it took him to light up and take a couple of puffs. "The fellow you'd want to ask is Charles Baxter. Man was obsessed with King Arthur. Don't misunderstand; he was a serious scholar, but he was far too eager to accept nonsense as possibly being true. Always sneaking around after dark with a metal detector. He hinted once or twice that he'd found something. Even claimed he'd explored that tunnel I mentioned."

Isla's heart raced. This Baxter fellow was exactly the man she needed to talk to.

Osbourne blew out a puff of smoke. "Of course, he's dead."

"That's too bad." Isla couldn't keep the disappointment out of her voice. "Does he have family in the area?"

"No idea. Anything else I can help you with?"

Isla shook her head. "Thank you for your time. You've been very kind."

"No problem. Walk you back to your car?"

"Thanks, but I'm going to spend some time here taking photos for the article."

Osborne bade her goodbye and headed back down the hill. Isla watched him go. She would, in fact, take a few photographs. After all, there would be an article to write. She needed her job and the credibility it afforded her. But her real work was just beginning.

CHAPTER 3
Caesar's Spring, Florida

Maddock settled into his folding camp chair, propped his feet on a rock, and closed his eyes. The dive had been refreshing, and left him tired, but it was the proverbial "good tired." The kind that left him relaxed at the end of a solid day's work.

"Beer?" Bones proffered a bottle of Dos Equis.

"Of course." Maddock accepted the drink, taking a moment to press its cool surface against his sweaty brow, letting the condensation drip down his face. It was a welcome relief in the humid Florida air.

"It goes in your mouth," Bones said.

Rolling his eyes, Maddock took a swig, then another. "This was a good idea," he said. "Thanks for suggesting it."

"Anything to get you to quit moping around your condo." Bones began laying a campfire. "As soon as we got back from Scotland you turned into an emo kid."

"Just got stuff on my mind." Maddock knew he'd been a hermit for the past several weeks but his friend had not been content to leave him alone. Although he and Angel had recently broken off their engagement, she wasn't foremost in his mind.

"Give it time. You and my sister will work things out." When Maddock didn't reply, Bones turned to look at him. "It is Angel you're moping about, isn't it?" His tone said it wasn't really a question.

"You know it is," Maddock lied. "We were together for a long time. It's just weird to be taking time off."

"I can't believe that, after all these years, I still haven't managed to teach you how to live." Bones lit the fire and sat back, watching the tiny flame grow into a cheery, crackling blaze. "This is a gift, Maddock. You can do anything you want, or anyone you…"

"I get it, Bones." Maddock took another drink.

"Do you?" Bones reached into the cooler and took

out another beer. "I'll make a deal with you. Take one month and pretend you're somebody else."

"Like who?"

"Like an ugly version of me." Bones grinned, took a drink, and let out a deep, protracted belch. "Panama City Beach is just down the road. College chicks galore. Let's go there, do a little partying, pick up some babes. No consequences."

"There are always consequences."

Bones turned and pointed at him. "That right there is what I'm talking about. You've been fifty years old since the day we met. Chill out for a few weeks. Live. After that, if you want to go back to being mister risk management, I'll leave you alone about it."

"The hell you will." Maddock chuckled. "But I'll think about it."

"I guess that's the best I can hope for." Bones cocked his head. "Somebody's coming. Not trying to be quiet about it, though."

"You and your hearing. I'm going to get a dog whistle just to annoy you." Still, Maddock reached down and grabbed the drawstring bag where his Walther was hidden.

A shadow appeared in the faint light, resolving into a decidedly feminine shape. As the figure drew closer, he recognized Nomi.

"Found you," she said. "I hope I'm not intruding."

"A hot chick is never an intrusion," Bones said. "Grab a chair and a beer." He handed her a bottle and pointed her to his own empty camp chair on the other side of the fire.

Nomi accepted both gratefully. "Thank you. I've been wandering this campground for an hour looking for you. It's sweaty work."

"You should have just asked someone where the hot guy and his little white friend were camping," Bones said.

"I should have, but I didn't want to disturb anyone."

Maddock eyed Nomi speculatively. He was still

convinced she was hiding something.

"Is this a social call?" he asked. "Because if it is, I can kick Bones' ass out of here for a couple of hours." If Bones wanted him to play a parody of a ladies' man, he could certainly give it a try.

"Not entirely." Nomi flashed him a sly grin. "I'm actually here on business."

"Now you've got Maddock's attention," Bones said. "Dude has no idea how to vacation. I invited him to Vegas and he wanted to know if there were any good museums."

"I like museums." Nomi flicked a grin Maddock's way.

"I see how it is," Bones grumbled. "So, what's this business you've got?"

When Nomi hesitated, Maddock said, "I assume it has something to do with the dive today?"

She nodded. "I wasn't honest with you about why I was there. Understand, I didn't know you at all. Actually, I still don't know you, but I've done some digging and your story checks out. You truly are former SEALs, quite accomplished, in fact. And you're treasure hunters. And then there are your more eccentric pursuits," she said to Bones. "The skunk ape? Honestly."

"No imagination." Bones winked at her.

Maddock hid his smile behind his bottle of beer. If the woman only knew half of what they'd seen and done.

"In any case," she went on, "I need to fully explore the passages connected to the spring and I can't do it alone. Will you help me?"

"What are we looking for?" Maddock asked.

"What's the pay?" Bones said at the same time.

"Let's say we're looking for my inheritance," she said carefully.

"We'll need a bit more information than that," Maddock said. He didn't like the woman's cagey style, but he'd been in the treasure hunting game long enough to know that suspicion ran rampant, and with good reason. It was a cutthroat business. Other treasure hunters thought nothing about scooping a find out from under your nose.

Nomi took a deep breath. "Have you heard of Black Caesar?"

Maddock sat up straight. Having been raised by a man who was obsessed with pirates, he had, indeed heard of the former slave turned buccaneer. "I have, but I don't know a great deal about him."

"He was Haitian, wasn't he?" Bones asked.

"You're thinking of Henri Caesar," Nomi said. "Some did, in fact, call him 'Black Caesar,' but he came along almost a century later. The man of whom I speak was a fearsome pirate who was hanged in 1718."

Maddock knew the general outline of Black Caesar's life. A fearsome warrior and charismatic leader during his days in Africa, he was enslaved through an act of deception. On his way across the Atlantic, he befriended one of the crew who later freed Caesar. The two made their escape on a lifeboat and began a life of piracy. Caesar eventually joined forces with the famed Blackbeard aboard the *Queen Anne's Revenge*, and served among the crew until his execution.

"So, Caesar's Spring is named after Black Caesar?" he asked.

"Yes. The name survived but the story behind it did not. The Florida Panhandle has not always been the sort of place where a site named for a black man would be something to crow about."

"And you think he hid treasure here?" Bones asked.

"Treasure and more. That he maintained a headquarters on Caesar's Rock near Key West is common knowledge, at least among those familiar with pirate lore. But my research indicates he also had an underground headquarters in this area, very close to Caesar's Spring. I've done enough searching to be satisfied that the main entrance has collapsed."

"What makes you think we can get to it by water?" Maddock asked.

"The few stories I could find all mention a spring-fed

pool in the headquarters. One large enough for him to drown his enemies in."

Maddock nodded, considering. "I don't know. The bedrock in this area is porous, so it's not a given that the pool, if it exists, would necessarily be connected to the spring."

"This land was privately owned until very recently, when the owner passed away," Nomi said. "The man who owned it was a scuba diving enthusiast in the 1980s. He privately claimed to have found a few gold coins in the spring. I did some checking and he did, in fact own three gold coins from the proper time period."

"You think a few bits of treasure drifted down the passageway over the centuries," Maddock said. "I suppose it's possible. Certainly worth investigating."

"So I ask again," Bones said, "what's the pay?"

"Half of any gold and jewels we find. I keep all artifacts of historical importance, plus any personal effects we might discover. If our search turns up nothing, we'll find a local bar and drown our sorrows on my dime."

"What do you say, Maddock?" Bones asked.

"Well, we did come here to do some diving."

"Works for me." Bones drained his beer and reached for the cooler. "There's one thing I don't like about this."

"What's that?" Maddock asked.

"I was really looking forward to heading to the beach and scamming on the college chicks."

CHAPTER 4
Glastonbury, England

Agnes Baxter, the widow of the deceased Charles Baxter, lived in a small cottage on a residential street in Glastonbury. It hadn't taken much searching for Isla to track her down. It had been a simple matter of getting her name from her husband's obituary, then looking her up in the local directory. Bless old people and their devotion to landlines.

She had decided not to call ahead. It was easier to tell someone "no" over the phone than in person. She'd simply do her best to charm the old woman. Painting on a smile, she rapped twice on the door.

"Who's there?" a sharp voice called.

"Isla Mulheron," she replied.

"You're a heron?" the voice asked. "What foolishness is that?"

"My name is Mulheron." This time she spoke slower and louder. "I'm here about your husband's research."

Silence.

Bloody hell. I've made a botch of it already. But then doorknob turned and the door opened a crack.

Rheumy blue eyes, unnaturally magnified by thick eyeglasses, peered up at her. "You say you're here about Charlie?"

Isla nodded. "I'm a writer for *Scottish Adventure* magazine. I'm doing a piece about Glastonbury Tor and Arthurian legend. I understand your husband was something of an expert."

Mrs. Baxter pursed her lips, her owlish gaze seeming to penetrate Isla. "I don't much care for the Scots. Difficult to understand you people."

Isla resisted the urge to roll her eyes. "I understand. I've lived in London and in New York, so my accent hopefully isn't too heavy."

"Don't much like reporters, either. Always misquoting you."

Isla was quickly losing hope. Over Mrs. Baxter's shoulder, she saw a television flickering. She recognized the person onscreen immediately.

"I'm working in conjunction with Grizzly Grant. Perhaps you've heard of him?"

"Grizzly" Don Grant was a television personality known for investigating ancient mysteries, legendary creatures, and bizarre conspiracy theories. Isla had recently written a series of articles about his investigations. Through that process she'd discovered that, in addition to being famous, he was also a buffoon. But Agnes Baxter did not know that.

"You know Grizzly?" Agnes shot a glance back at the television.

"I do. Let me show you." She took out her smartphone and called up a photograph. It was taken on the shore of Loch Ness. Isla stood by the water, flanked by Grizzly on one side and two men on the other—a handsome blond and a massive Native American. Dane Maddock and Bones Bonebrake. The sight of Maddock's blue eyes caused the back of her throat to pinch, and she hastily stretched the image so that only she and Grizzly were visible. She held it up for the old woman to see.

Mrs. Baxter's countenance changed in an instant. She smiled, shuffled backward, and opened the door.

"Please come inside. Grizzly is just wonderful, don't you think?"

"He is quite the character," she said.

The house was brightly lit, and smelled of lemon-scented cleaner. Agnes, as she insisted Isla call her, ushered her to a dining room table and busied herself preparing tea.

"How long have you known Grizzly?" she asked. "I have been watching his programs for years."

"Only a few months, actually. We did an investigation of the Old Gray Man, and another of Loch Ness."

"Scotland." Agnes' tone underscored her opinion of the Scots. After several minutes of preparation, she served up strong tea and a plate of biscuits. Isla hadn't eaten today and had to restrain herself from devouring them.

"What is it you want to know about Charlie's work?" Agnes took a sip of her tea and stared intently at Isla.

"My readers and Grizzly's viewers are interested in local legends that connect King Arthur or any of his knights to the tor. I was told your husband was an expert on such things."

Agnes smiled. "Some might call it expertise; others called it eccentricity. But yes, he gathered many such stories."

Isla drank her tea while Agnes summarized the familiar legends surrounding the tor. Arthur once freed Guinevere from a fortress at the summit. Arthur was brought to the tor to heal after the final battle. Glastonbury was the site of Avalon. She had heard all of these before but wanted Agnes to warm up to the subject and hopefully let down her guard, so she smiled, asked a few questions, and took notes.

"Have there been any archaeological finds connecting the site to Arthur?"

"You mean aside from the discovery of the bodies of Arthur and Guinevere?"

The story rang a bell with Isla, but she wanted Agnes to keep talking. "I haven't heard about that."

"In 1191, acting on information given to King Henry II by an elderly bard, the monks at Glastonbury excavated a spot between two stone pyramids. Far below the surface they uncovered a hollowed-out log containing two bodies. One was a large man with a severe head injury, the other a woman with long hair. Along with it they found a stone slab, or a cross, depending on which story you believe, naming the deceased as Arthur and Guinevere."

"Inside a log, you say?"

"That was not unusual for Arthur's time period. At least, that's what my husband told me. There's a marker showing the site where the bodies were found."

"What happened to their bodies?" Isla asked.

"No one knows. They were removed sometime before the dissolution of the abbey in 1539."

"You said the bodies were buried between pyramids? Odd, isn't it?"

Agnes dismissed the question with a wave of an arthritic hand. "That's not the oddest bit." She lowered her voice, as if afraid someone might hear. "My husband says the bodies were not those of Arthur and Guinevere. In fact, they were not human at all. At least, no human he'd ever seen."

"What did he mean by that?"

"The skeletons were exceptionally tall; taller than the tallest man, and their eyes were huge and widely spaced."

Isla nodded, her thoughts racing. If the skeletons were alien, then the artifact she sought could be alien in origin. But there was something else that had caught her attention. "At least, no human he'd ever seen." Charles Baxter had seen these skeletons, and if she did not miss her guess, that meant they were still somewhere in the area.

"Did your husband mention any legends about a secret passageway beneath the abbey? Perhaps one that led to the tor?" When Agnes didn't reply, she pressed further. "Or any legends about Launcelot?"

Agnes set her cup down on the table and slowly sat up straight. "You are looking for the Sword Bridge."

Something about her demeanor told Isla to proceed with caution. In the background, the television flickered. She heard Grizzly droning on about a monster in New Jersey.

"It's just something Grizzly wanted me to ask about. He didn't go into any detail."

Once again, the mention of the television host put Agnes at ease. "The villain, Maleagant, abducted Guinevere and took her to an island made of crystal, accessible only by the Sword Bridge. Some legends say Glastonbury Tor was that island. The Celtic name for it translates to Isle of Glass."

"What happened to Guinevere?"

"Launcelot came to her rescue. He used a magic ring to defeat Maleagant and save the queen."

It took all of Isla's will to maintain her composure. This was exactly what she had been sent to find.

"Did your husband ever find a magic ring?" She'd blurted the question out before she'd realized what she was doing. But it had the desired effect.

Caught off guard, Agnes blurted, "Yes, but he didn't keep it."

"What did he do with it?"

"He put it back where it belonged. It was a holy object."

Isla frowned. "Holy to whom? Pagans?"

Agnes shook her head. "My dear, you have the wrong idea. The ring was brought to England by Joseph of Arimathea."

Isla's head spun as she tried to connect the legends of the Red Spring with the Arthurian myths. Was Agnes conflating myths, or had Nineve sent Isla off in search of a Biblical artifact?"

"This is all fascinating. Can you tell me where he put the ring? I'd love to see it."

Agnes shook her head.

"Did he put it with the skeletons?" She hoped another direct question might rattle some useful information out of Agnes, but this time it did not work.

"I will not tell you where it is."

"I promise I'm not out to steal it. I won't even tell Grizzly about it if you don't want me to." She hated being forced to drop Grizzly's name, but it was the last bullet in her gun.

"It's not a matter of trust or secrecy. It's about keeping you alive. The Sword Bridge killed my husband."

"What do you mean?"

Agnes took a long time to answer. Tears, magnified to pearlescent marbles, welled behind her lenses and spilled down her cheeks.

"He was a young man when he found the ring, and he managed all right. But when he decided to replace it…" She shook her head. "I told him he was too old, but he insisted. When he came home there was something different about him. Died in his sleep that very night."

"I'm so sorry." Isla reached across the table to take the old woman's hand, but she pulled away. "This probably won't make any sense to you, but I have to at least try and find the ring. I can't explain why, but I'm going to do it. Can you tell me anything that can help me?"

Agnes sighed, and then fixed Isla with a pitying look that said the woman expected she'd never see Isla again.

"I only know what my husband said. He used to repeat it, like a mantra. 'Follow the stony path. The bridge is real. The lions are not.' That's all I know. Now I would appreciate it if you would leave."

Isla thanked Agnes, who saw her to the door in stony silence. Outside, Isla took a moment to consider what she'd learned. The ring was real, and she had a feeling she knew where to look for it.

CHAPTER 5
Caesar's Spring, Florida

The tunnel was pitch black, the confines cramped, but to Maddock it felt like being wrapped in a warm blanket. He loved these sorts of places, free from the distractions of the real world. Perhaps that made him odd, but what of it? It was a quality that allowed him to plumb depths that many would not risk. Countless times he'd seen others turn back or even panic due to claustrophobia or the inability to tolerate the utter lack of light and sound.

Bringing up the rear, he paused to secure a directional marker to their reel line. This was, in fact, their third line. It was a risky proposition, delving this deep, but this was the only passage that hadn't become impassable after a short distance. Perhaps this one would be a winner.

He clipped the arrow-shaped marker onto the line, then turned to follow Bones and Nomi. He didn't have to follow far. Up ahead, the two had come to a halt.

Bones turned toward Maddock, shook his head, and drew a finger across his throat. *Another dead end.*

Maddock raised his palms as if to say, *are you sure?*

Bones held his hands a few inches apart. *Too narrow.*

For some reason, this did not sit well with Maddock. Ordinarily, the confines would gradually constrict until a diver could no longer squeeze through. This change seemed sudden. Curious, he swam forward to take a closer look.

The opening up ahead was, in fact, too narrow for any of them to squeeze through. But as he scrutinized it, he realized the way was blocked by fallen chunks of stone. Silt and debris had accumulated in the cracks—enough to give the illusion of solidity. Getting the others' attention, he shone his light on a spot and gently probed it with his knife, being careful not to stir up too much silt.

Bones nodded in understanding, then pointed at the ceiling and cocked his head. The question was clear. *Will we cause a collapse if we try to move it?*

This was new. Bones being the cautious one?

Nomi appeared to understand. She pointed at the rocks and nodded.

Maddock now gave the spot a second look. Bones' caution had caused him to reconsider. Perhaps it was too risky. What if nothing lay beyond except more darkness? He directed his light through the narrow opening and his breath caught in his throat.

Not more than ten meters beyond, a pile of skulls grinned back at him.

They needed no more convincing. Carefully, he and Bones began removing the debris. It wasn't long before minute particles filled the water, rendering visibility nil. They labored as if working in a blizzard, only able to see a few inches in front of their faces. After three very long, tense minutes, they had cleared enough of a path for the three of them to swim through.

Maddock went last, playing out the last of their line. It was a tight fit. Bones had scarcely squeezed through, and Maddock, though not as massive as his friend, was broad of shoulder. He proceeded with caution, trying not to knock anything loose. As he slipped through, he heard a dull knocking sound, and something grabbed him by the fin.

He looked back to see that a large chunk of rock had fallen, catching the tip of his fin and partially blocking their way out. Nomi could probably squeeze through, but it would have to be moved before he or Bones could pass. Carefully, he worked himself free and rejoined his companions.

Nomi was enthusiastically pointing out various marks on the skeletal bits that lay partially covered in silt. Deep grooves in the rib cage of one skeleton, indicating the victim had been stabbed in the heart. Skulls with gaping holes in the back. Maddock understood the reason for her excitement. These people had been executed, lending credence to the Black Caesar legend she had uncovered.

He looked up above and saw the surface of the water shimmering ten meters above. He pointed up to it. Bones and Nomi nodded and, as one, they swam upward.

Breaking the surface, Maddock saw that they were at the end of a narrow cave. The far end was blocked by a mountain of rubble, but it was what lay in between that caught his eye.

"Gold," Bones said. "Hell, yes!"

To the left, a pile of gold lay spilled out on the floor amidst the rotting remains of the chest that had once held it. To their right stood a small armory—rusted swords, a couple of flintlock pistols, and a small keg of powder. Next to that stood a crudely built wooden table and a few chairs.

Maddock spat out his regulator and took a tentative breath. The air was stale but breathable.

"This is it ," he said.

"I'm first," Nomi said.

"Hold on." Maddock laid a hand on her shoulder. "I understand, but this is a pirate's den. There might be booby traps."

"I think you've seen too many adventure movies," Nomi said.

"Trust me."

"Let me guess," Bones said. "You want me to check it out."

"You're the most expendable...I mean, dependable."

"Screw you, Maddock." Bones took a long look around, checking the floor and ceiling. Maddock did the same. There didn't seem to be anything there that might endanger them.

"I have a feeling that Caesar would only have rigged the entrance," Maddock said. "Just watch your step." Patches of sand and fine gravel lay here and there, but the floor was mostly clean and featureless. No signs of trapdoors or steps that might trigger something dangerous.

"Been there, done that." Bones heaved his bulk out of the water and clambered into the cave. He stripped off his fins, then, dripping water, he made a circuit of the cavern. "Looks clear to me, but enter at your own risk."

"Good enough." Nomi climbed out, followed by Maddock. Maddock and Bones removed their fins and air tanks and stowed them in a nearby alcove. Nomi left her gear on, mesmerized by their surroundings.

While Bones knelt over the small treasure pile, taking inventory, Maddock took in the entirety of the cavern. The hollowed out cupboard that would have held food stores. The broken remnants of rum barrels. Shards of crockery. The graffiti-like carvings on the wall. As much as he loved finding treasure, it was the historical aspect that fascinated him the most. He tried to imagine himself a pirate, holed up in this cave. Carousing, singing, planning their next raid.

He began snapping photographs, recording every inch of the site before they disturbed it. He wished his dad could see it. A lump formed in his throat. Even after all these years, there were still moments when he would forget the accident, and a wave of grief would wash over him anew.

"You all right, Maddock?" Bones asked.

"Yep."

"Cool. Listen, don't take any photos of the treasure pile until I've taken our finder's fee."

Shaking his head, Maddock turned away.

"Don't argue with me, dude. We've got more right to this treasure than the government does. Wasn't one of their agencies that found it."

"I'm not going to look. Plausible deniability, you know." If the cave was located on public land, which Maddock suspected it was, considering the direction and distance they had traveled, the law held that all of the treasure belonged to the state. Common practice was for the state to keep all artifacts of historical value, and give the finders a share of any treasure. There was, however, no guarantee. "Just leave enough so it doesn't look suspicious," he said.

"I know what I'm doing. A little for us, a little for Nomi. Hey Nomi, do you want some of these jewels, or just some gold?"

"Doesn't matter," Nomi said absently. Her attention was focused on whatever lay on the table.

Maddock turned and took a few steps in her direction, but sprang back when a loud crack echoed through the cave.

"What the hell was that?" Bones asked.

"The floor isn't solid. At least, not everywhere. Watch your step."

"We're not all as fat as you, Maddock," Bones said, returning to bagging gold coins.

"Whatever." Maddock shone his light on the spot that had nearly given way. A strange pattern caught his eye. The carving was shallow, easy to miss. But he recognized it immediately, and it didn't belong here. He took out his camera and took photos from several angles, then knelt and brushed away the sand to make sure he hadn't missed anything.

"I can't believe this!" Nomi shouted. Maddock turned to see the young woman slam her fist down on the table. The aged, rotting wood splintered beneath the blow. "That's just wonderful," she muttered, looking down at the hole she'd punched in its surface.

"What's going on?" Bones asked.

"It's ruined." She held up a leather bound journal. "I finally found Black Caesar's journal and the pages are stuck together, the ink smeared. It's a mess."

"Maybe some of the pages can be salvaged," Maddock said. "Some labs can…"

"I don't want to hear about it," she snapped. "You can't possibly know how it feels to come this far and…" She looked up, glowered at the ceiling. "Forget it. Perhaps some of these other papers will be of use." She took out a waterproof bag and stowed the journal and various papers. Next, she double-bagged it, then secured the bundle in a larger dive bag.

"Here's your gold," Bone said. "Consolation prize?"

"Thanks." She tucked the gold into the bag. Head down, she stalked toward the pool through which they'd entered the cave.

"You sure you're ready to go? Don't want to look around a little longer?" Maddock asked. He wanted to give the strange carving a closer inspection.

"There's nothing else here for me. Thank you for your help."

"Hold on, chick," Bones said. "Give us a minute."

Nomi smirked, reached into a pouch at her belt, and pulled out something the size of her fist.

"Sorry, gentlemen, but you're not coming with me." She tossed the object on the ground and plunged into the water.

Maddock didn't get a good look at what she'd dropped, but somehow he knew what it was.

"Grenade!"

He dove for cover as the world around him erupted in fire and smoke.

CHAPTER 6
Glastonbury Abbey

Beneath the cover of darkness, Isla crept about the ruins of Glastonbury Abbey. Founded in the seventh century, the abbey was destroyed by fire in 1184 and rebuilt in the fourteenth century. It had once numbered among the richest and most powerful monasteries in England, controlling large swathes of land and exerting great influence over the local populace until its dissolution under King Henry VIII. Isla had seen replicas in miniature of Glastonbury in its glory and found it hard to believe that so little remained of the once-great monastery.

The ruins stood in the midst of a wide swathe of manicured green space. She crossed it hastily, feeling vulnerable out in the open, until she reached the site of King Arthur's grave. She had to confess it was something of a disappointment—a rectangular area marked by a sign. Kneeling before it, dew soaking the knees of her jeans, she read the words lettered in white. The sign marked this as the spot upon which the bodies of Arthur and Guinevere had been excavated and gave a few details of the treatment of the remains. There was nothing here that Agnes had not already told her.

She sighed. This was a dead end. If there had been a tunnel here, it was buried long ago. It could not possibly be the spot Baxter had found. The entrance had to be somewhere among the ruins.

She made her way toward the dark, hulking outline of the old monastery. As she walked, she felt an itch at the center of her back, and the feeling someone was watching her. She knew it was foolish. This wasn't the sort of place that required high-level security, and on a foggy night such as this, she was nearly invisible as long as she didn't turn on her torch.

She started with the ruins of the Great Church, where only a few sections of masonry survived from the nave and transepts of the old structure. It didn't take long to satisfy herself that there was nothing to find here. Next she moved on to the Lady Chapel.

Built immediately after the fire that consumed the abbey in the late twelfth century, the chapel remained largely intact. Despite her anxiety, Isla could not help but take time to admire its design. The ornate capitals that crested the various columns, the arches adorned with chevrons, and the portals with elaborate floral sculptures made it a striking example of Early English architecture. As she wandered the ruin, however, she couldn't shake the perpetual chill that soaked her to the bone. It was more than the cool, damp air. In the scant light, the shadowy ruin felt like a haunted house. She half expected the ghost of a headless nun to come floating around the corner. The mental image made her laugh, the sound unnaturally shrill in the quiet night.

Get a grip on yourself. You've got a job to do.

She descended to the lower level of the chapel's interior. Here, below ground level and shielded by stone walls, she felt comfortable turning on her torch. Though she walked softly, the sound of her trainers treading upon flagstones sounded like a steady drumbeat. She wished she had someone keeping a lookout. Even a moron like Grizzly would provide a measure of comfort. Perhaps she wasn't as self-reliant as she'd always believed.

She took her time exploring the chapel's dark recesses, searching for anything that might be an entrance to a secret tunnel. She tested the walls and floor for hollow spaces, looked for unusual markings that might point the way. Nothing. Finally, she was forced to admit that this place, too, was a dead end.

She checked her watch. It was after midnight; several hours of darkness remained. Unfortunately, she was running out of places to search. Unless, of course the entrance was in some obscure location, like beneath one of the nearby ponds. If she didn't find something soon, she'd have to go back and try to prise some more information out of Agnes. Or maybe Mr. Baxter had left records of his research behind. If Isla could slip into the house unnoticed...

What was she thinking? Breaking into an elderly woman's house in order to try and steal something that might not exist? What was wrong with her?

"That's an ironic train of thought, considering you're presently trespassing on a scheduled monument in hopes of finding a secret path that will lead you to a magic ring owned by a figure out of legend." She said the words aloud, savoring the absurdity. Then again, she had recently taken part in a search for relics that had proved to be exactly as legend described them.

Exiting the chapel, she paused to look around. She still appeared to have the place to herself. If there was a security guard on duty, he was most likely somewhere inside where it was warm and dry. Probably enjoying a nice cuppa. She imagined sitting before a cheery fire, a piping hot mug in her hands. The thought made the night seem that much colder. When had she become so weak? Annoyed, she stalked out onto the grass, looking around for a likely spot to search.

Her eyes fell upon the Abbot's Kitchen, an octagonal building that abutted a small section of the ruined wall that had once been a part of the opulent Abbot's Hall. Unlike the other sections of the abbey, the structure remained intact. It was considered one of the best preserved medieval kitchens in all of Europe. Isla didn't consider it a promising possibility. She knew from research that the interior had been set up to replicate a functioning kitchen, and that the site saw significant foot traffic every day. It seemed to her unlikely that a secret passageway could go undiscovered in such a spot.

Sighing, she gazed at the dark outline of the kitchen. A sliver of moonlight peeked through the clouds, casting a silver glow upon the buttresses that supported the walls, each leading up to a cornice adorned with grotesque gargoyles. It was certainly mysterious-looking, with its blocky, fortress-like base and pyramidal roof.

She froze. Pyramids had once flanked Arthur's burial site. Add in the Middle Eastern connection to Joseph of Arimathea, and it suddenly seemed possible that the kitchen could, in fact, be the place she was looking for. Heart racing, she made her way over to the dark building.

The door was locked. Why this came as a surprise to her she had no idea. She jiggled the handle, as if that would make a difference, and even tried throwing her weight against it. All she got for her trouble was a sore shoulder and bruised ego. Damn! She should have learned how to pick locks. Bones had boasted about his skill, said it was easy to learn. She couldn't let her attempt be foiled by one locked door. There had to be another way in.

She rounded the building, searching for another point of ingress. She was halfway around when her foot struck something solid. She stumbled, barely catching herself before she fell on her face.

"What the hell was that?"

Not willing to risk using her torch, she took out her smartphone and tapped the screen. The faint glow was sufficient to reveal what lay in the grass before her. A cellar door!

"Now, that seems like just the thing."

She released the simple latch that held the door closed, raised it, and shined her light inside. She could tell immediately that this was part of the original structure. It had been converted to a storage space at some point in the past, but not too recently, considering the layer of dust that coated everything. Smiling, she climbed down into the cellar and closed the door behind her.

She flicked on her torch, the sudden burst of light stinging her eyes. It was a small space, the ceiling only a few inches above her head. Sagging cardboard boxes were stacked against the wall to her left. Cobweb-coated rakes and shovels stood on her right. A cursory inspection of the space revealed nothing promising. But then, something caught her attention.

Where most of the boxes were roughly stacked, most collapsing from the weight of those above them, one section stood out. Here, the boxes were in better condition, arranged in straight columns, and even a bit less dusty than their counterparts. It was almost as if they'd been arranged that way for a specific purpose. Holding her torch in her teeth, she began moving the boxes until finally, at the base of the wall, she uncovered a roughly hewn stone, circular in shape, the faint image of a dragon carved in its surface. A rusted iron ring hung from the dragon's nose. She took hold of it, its pitted surface cold against her flesh, and pulled.

CHAPTER 7
Caesar's Spring

Maddock covered his ears as the grenade boomed inside the cave. Sheltered inside a cleft in the wall, he none the less felt the effects of the blast. Flying fragments of rock sliced into his back and debris rained down on him from above. The floor vibrated beneath his feet and he winced, waiting for the ceiling to collapse.

After a few seconds of tense waiting, he opened his eyes and uncovered his ringing ears. Smoke filled the cave and the floor was covered with rocks and debris, but it remained structurally sound. He took a step and felt the floor crack. All right. It was sound for the moment.

"Bones?" he called tentatively. He had no idea where his friend had taken shelter.

The beam of his dive lamp sliced through the smoke, a fine line of white in the choking darkness. It was like ground zero. The furnishings, already half-rotten, had been blown to splinters. The rusted weapons were shattered. Even the pool through which they'd entered the cave was now covered with debris. Everything was gone.

Including Bones.

"Bones! Where the hell are you?"

Maddock hurried from one pile of rubble to another, pushing debris aside, searching for a sign of his friend.

"Yell, groan, say something so I can find you," he called to the darkness.

In response, a large hand poked out from the flotsam-choked pool. Then another. Seconds later, Bones heaved his bulk out into the cavern, rolled onto his back, and lay looking up at the ceiling.

"Was that you yelling?" he panted. "You weren't worried about me, were you?"

"I was afraid you were lying unconscious somewhere and I'd have to haul you out." Maddock couldn't hide the relief from his voice. "Risky move, diving into the water like that."

"You know me. I jump first and think about it later. It shielded me from the blast, but a whole hell of a lot of ceiling came crashing down on me. I barely got out."

"Can we get back out that way?" Maddock asked.

"Not a chance."

Maddock helped Bones to his feet and the two men inspected the cave. There was no longer anything to see except rubble.

"Not much left," Bones said. "But I did manage to hold on to our share of the gold. The weight made it harder to swim out again, but I wasn't leaving here empty-handed."

"Assuming we can get out of here at all." Maddock continued his examination of the cave, but he could see no means of egress.

"Always the pessimist." Bones folded his arms and scowled at the small, blackened crater where the grenade had gone off. "Why do you think she did it? It wasn't about the treasure. She had her half, and killing us wouldn't get her our share. As soon as she bagged up that ruined journal, she booked it out of here."

"I can't say for certain, but I think it has something to do with this." Maddock moved to the spot where he'd seen the strange carving on the ground, knelt, and cleared away the debris to reveal a pair of interlocked triangles forming a six-pointed star, surrounded by a circle and six dots. "Do you recognize this?"

"Star of David?" Bones asked.

"Close. The Star of David was inspired by this symbol."

"Maddock, we're in a cave that might collapse at any time. How about you belay the suspense and just tell me what the hell it is?"

"It's Solomon's Seal."

"As in King Solomon? Dude with a thousand smoking hot wives?"

"Not quite that many, but he did have a ton of them. I doubt all of them were hot."

Bones shook his head. "Why do you always have to ruin things for me, Maddock?" He paused, scratched his chin. "So, what's the connection between Black Caesar and King Solomon?"

"I don't know, but this has to run deeper than a woman tracking down a pirate lair, and a conspiracy involving Solomon would fit the bill. She definitely wouldn't want experienced treasure hunters on the trail."

Bones' eyes lit up. "You're talking about King Solomon's mines?"

"That's what my gut tells me. For what it's worth, I don't think Nomi saw this carving. I think she hoped the journal would lead her to the mines. When that didn't happen, she left, and tried to kill us just to be safe."

A sharp crack rang out and Maddock danced sideways as a hunk of rock fell. It struck the floor where he'd stood moments before and shattered.

"What's our play?" Bones asked. "We could try to clear the pool, but my hopes aren't high."

Maddock had a different idea. "I want to try something." He took a few steps and paused when he felt the floor crack beneath his feet. *Here goes nothing.* He raised his foot and stamped down.

Crack!

Pain shot up his leg. For a moment, he'd forgotten he wasn't wearing shoes. *Brilliant, Maddock.*

He took a step back, raised his foot, and repeated the action.

Crack!

And then the floor gave way beneath his feet. He felt himself falling, but Bones caught him from behind and hauled him back.

"I get what you're doing," Bones said, "but there's no guarantee there's water down there. Might be another cave."

"Good point." Cautiously, Maddock looked down into the hole he'd created. A few feet below the surface his light reflected off of dark water. This entire region was a honeycomb of underwater tunnels. He was gambling that they could find one that would lead them to safety.

"It's a risk," Bones said. "We get down there and find out it's a dead end, we're screwed."

"Not necessarily. We'll keep an eye on our air. Worst case, we come back here and try to dig our way out."

Bones nodded. "It's your brilliant idea. You go first."

"Fine."

They recovered their gear and suited up. Maddock wondered if they were doing the right thing. Possibly they would accomplish no more than waste precious air.

"Anytime, Maddock."

Maddock was about to suggest they take one more look for a way out when the decision was taken out of his hands by a low rumble and the crack of the ceiling above them shattering. The place was coming down around them. Cursing inwardly, he plunged into the icy water.

The two men hit the water simultaneously and began to swim. All around them, chunks of stone fell through the water. One caught Maddock on the back of the head and he saw stars, but kept on swimming. The dark passageway curved to the left, looping back in the direction of the spring. But Maddock's rising hope was quickly dashed as he rounded a corner and hit a dead end. This was it. They couldn't keep going and couldn't go back to the cave. He'd led them to their death.

Damn!

In frustration he punched the wall in front of him. The brittle limestone shattered, revealing a familiar-looking passageway up ahead. There was their guide rope! Eroded by the flow of water over time, the wall he'd struck had been wafer-thin. It was only due to dumb luck, but he'd saved them.

By the time they returned to the surface, their tanks were nearing empty. They paused to catch their breath, enjoying the fresh air and sunlight.

"Not bad," Bones said. "Usually, I'm the one saving our asses by breaking stuff."

"I learned from the best." Maddock took a moment

to reflect on the day's events. They'd gone from a simple dive in search of the lair of an obscure pirate, to almost being killed. And if his guess was correct, they were now on the trail of one of the greatest treasures in history. He turned to Bones. "I know we're supposed to be on vacation, but I'm in the mood for a treasure hunt. How about you?"

Bones smiled. "Glad to see you getting back to normal. I'd also like to see if we can find out who Nomi really is and who she works for."

"I've got some ideas on both counts."

"Works for me, but it'll have to wait until tomorrow. I've got other plans."

"Like what?"

"Like rewarding attractive young ladies for their patriotism." He pointed off to their right, where the two young women they'd seen the previous day lay sunbathing. They'd traded their Confederate flag bikinis for the stars and stripes.

"That's technically a violation of the flag code," Maddock said with mock sincerity.

"I agree. They should take those suits off immediately."

Maddock rolled his eyes. Some things never changed.

CHAPTER 8
Glastonbury Abbey

Isla found herself staring down a long, sloping stone passageway. Crumbling stonework lined the walls and ceiling. Dust covered the flagstone floor. The corridor was coated in enough cobwebs to decorate a haunted house. This place had been here for a long time.

She immediately noticed that there was something odd about the path that lay in front of her. The layer of dust was noticeably thinner in the center, as if someone had passed this way before. Not too long ago, but long enough that a new layer had begun to form. But why was it so uniform? Footsteps wouldn't do that. It was as if something heavy had been dragged across the floor. Then she remembered what Agnes had said.

When he came home there was something different about him. Died in his sleep that very night.

She had visions of Charles Baxter, dying from whatever the Sword Bridge had done to him, dragging himself up the gentle slope toward the door. She'd had her doubts when Agnes had shared that particular story, but now she wasn't so certain.

Intent on exercising caution, she dug into her drawstring bag and took out gloves and a dust mask. It was entirely possible that in an ancient tunnel like this one, Baxter had been exposed to some sort of deadly spores. No telling what kinds of mold grew down here. Next, she pocketed her flashlight and strapped on a headlamp. Best to have both hands free. Finally ready, she clambered into the passageway. She debated closing the door behind her, but if anyone followed her into the cellar, they'd see the boxes she'd moved and know exactly where she'd gone. No sense risking it locking behind her. She propped it open with one of the old boxes and descended into the darkness.

The passage leveled out and soon branched off in three directions. She took a moment to inspect them.

Nothing seemed amiss about any of them—no obvious traps or pitfalls. The only obvious difference was the floor. The branch to the left had a dirt floor, the one straight ahead was of crumbling brick, the path to the right the same stone as that on which she stood.

It's too easy, she thought. One's natural inclination would be to stay on the flagstones and ignore these other two passages. But what was the clue Agnes had passed along?

Follow the stony path. The bridge is real; the lions are not.

"Charles Baxter, you'd better not have been lying," she said to the darkness as she turned and followed the way to her right. She proceeded with caution, testing the ground with each step before putting her weight forward, looking for anything that might be a booby trap. After a few minutes of this, she allowed herself to relax. After all, Baxter hadn't said anything to his wife about any traps. Or, if he had, Agnes hadn't passed it along. She hoped it was the former.

She turned a corner and found herself face-to-face with a lion. She let out a high-pitched yelp and sprang back, banging her head against the wall behind her. She held out her hands in a futile defensive gesture, but the lion didn't move.

"It's a statue, you eejit," she scolded herself. "Baxter said it. The lions are not real."

But it certainly looked real enough. The creature was sculpted in remarkable detail and painted to add to the realism. For some reason, it wasn't covered in dust. As she looked around, she realized the same was true of the entire chamber in which she stood. Up ahead, she heard a whispering sound, like the rush of water, and felt a hint of a breeze.

She skirted the lion, eyeing it suspiciously, as if it might spring to life at any moment. On the other side an arched doorway led to a steep path that wound down to a dark crevasse. She descended the damp, slippery rocks with caution, not relishing the idea of a tumble through the darkness. A few meters from the bottom her footing slipped. Her feet shot out from under her and she hit the ground with a jarring thud. She half-rolled, half-slid, the rest of the way down, the beam of her headlamp playing crazily about.

Strobelike images flashed in front of her as she rolled, and then the dark chasm loomed before her, coming closer as she slid across the slick ground. She dug her fingers into the stone floor and felt the sharp stab of pain as fingernails tore free as she tried desperately to gain purchase on the slick surface. She dug in with her toes, braking her slide. She let out a cry that was half fear, half defiance, and skidded to a halt with her head hanging over the side of the ledge. The beam of her lamp pierced the darkness, its light dancing on the water far below.

"Oh my God, that was too close." She took a moment to catch her breath before carefully scooting back away from the edge and regaining her feet. The cavern in which she stood was no more than twenty meters wide and about the same distance across. Filling most of that space was the deep defile into which she'd nearly fallen. Two bridges stood before her. The one to the left appeared to be hewn from the native stone in the shape of a massive lion in mid-leap. A narrow set of steps ran up its hind legs, along its back, over its head, and down to a ledge on the far side.

To her right lay a much less solid looking structure. It was a long, tapered, glassy-looking path. A groove ran down the center and its edges were razor sharp, like the blade of a sword.

"The Sword Bridge," she whispered. "It's real."

Though it sparkled crystalline beneath the glow of her headlamp, it absolutely did not look like something she wanted to put her full weight on, much less try to walk across. Aside from the fact it was barely wide enough for her to walk on and coated in condensation, it was thin, much too thin to bear weight. The surface was cracked and pitted.

"I can't possibly walk across that thing."

She moved to the lion bridge. It appeared solid enough. But she couldn't forget Baxter's warning.

The bridge is real; the lions are not.

"Lions" plural. He wasn't only speaking of the life-like statue that guarded the way and this was the only other lion she had seen. Was this a trick to trip up the unwary? Was the Sword Bridge sturdier than it looked? Would the lion crumble beneath her feet? Kneeling to inspect it, she immediately saw cracks like spider webs covering every inch of its surface. She knocked and was rewarded with a hollow echo. She grimaced. Despite outward appearances, this bridge was not solid. She imagined it would shatter within a few steps.

"The Sword Bridge it is." Saying the words aloud did nothing to assuage her fears. The thing didn't look sturdy. But it had supported Baxter's weight, hadn't it? Indiana Jones had faced something like this—a transparent bridge, invisible in his case. He'd concluded it was a leap of faith, and stepped out into the chasm.

"Screw that." She took a rope out of her pack, secured one end to the largest boulder she could find, and tied the other end around her waist. It might just save her life if she should fall. Assuming, of course, the razor-sharp edge of the Sword Bridge didn't slice it in two. "Such happy thoughts."

As a last measure, she found a heavy stone and pushed it out on to the bridge. Everything held firm. Nothing shattered or even cracked.

"That thing doesn't weigh as much as you," she reminded herself. But what else could she do except give it a go and see what happened? She could turn back, she supposed. "No way. Maddock wouldn't turn back."

This time she felt no sadness at the thought of Maddock. Only anger. Here she was, standing in front of the Sword Bridge, something every bit as legendary as Nessie or the treasures of the Tuatha de Danaan, and she was thinking about a man. No more foolishness. It was time to move.

She took a step out onto the bridge and gingerly shifted her weight forward.

It held.

Another step, then a big step up and over the boulder she'd pushed out onto the bridge. That decision now seemed foolish as she overbalanced and fell forward with a scream. She landed flat on her stomach, the breath leaving her in a huff.

Up ahead, a dull popping sound, and then something whizzed through the air, zipping past her and vanishing into the darkness. Some sort of dart, if she didn't miss her guess, and if she'd been standing, it would have struck her full-on.

"Found the booby trap," she wheezed. She lay there until she managed to catch her breath, and then continued on. Discretion being the better part of valor, she continued to scoot forward on her belly, snakelike, in case there were more darts in the offing, but none came.

She reached the other side without incident, freed herself from her safety rope, and stood. To her left, the ledge came to a dead end, but to her right, a narrow cleft in the rock led into the darkness. She chose this path, hoping no more traps lay in her path.

She squeezed through the narrow passageway and came out in a tiny cave, barely larger than her first flat in New York City. The space was dominated by two massive stone coffins. Taking out her camera and her torch, she crept closer.

Agnes had warned her what to expect, but seeing it for herself sent a shiver of excitement down her spine. Two skeletons, each taller and broader of hip and shoulder, lay in silent repose. Their oversized eye sockets stared up at the ceiling. She began snapping photographs from every angle. She had no idea what she'd do with them. The Sisterhood wanted certain artifacts, but seemed not to care about any other aspect of history. Would her magazine print them? Would Nineve even permit her to share this part of the story, or would she insist that this mysterious tomb be kept a secret?

"What are you?" she whispered to the larger skeleton. "Alien? Nephilim? Anunnaki? You're not King Arthur, that's for bloody certain. No wonder the church wanted you hidden. You don't fit the narrative."

Satisfied she'd gotten more than enough photos, she put her camera away.

"Now, where did Baxter put that ring?"

There it was, around the fourth finger of the giant's left hand. She slipped it off of the bony finger and held it up to the light. It was unremarkable, really. A simple golden signet ring featuring an engraved cross. No, not a cross; an Ankh—the Egyptian symbol for eternal life.

"I doubt the Lady of the Lake gave you to Launcelot, but you just might be Middle Eastern." Smiling, she sealed the ring into a bag, put it in her backpack, and headed for the bridge.

"To hell with you, Dane Maddock," she muttered. "I can solve ancient mysteries without you."

CHAPTER 9
Key West, Florida

Maddock parked his 1975 Ford Bronco in front of Avery Halsey's building and climbed out. He'd caught an early flight to Miami and driven the rest of the way to Key West. He was exhausted, and not just from travel, but hope buoyed his spirits. Maybe, just maybe, Avery would have something for him.

He took the stairs two at a time and headed to the only apartment with a maple leaf sticker adorning the window. Avery opened the door just as Maddock raised his fist to knock. Her blue eyes peered out at him through the crack. "Got you again."

"Why exactly do you find that so amusing?" Maddock asked as his sister swung the door wide to let him in.

"Because, whenever I do it, you get that annoyed look on your face. That, and I missed out on pestering you as a kid, so I'm making up for it now."

Maddock chuckled and gave his sister a quick hug. Though they had the same father, Maddock had grown up in Florida, Avery in Nova Scotia. He had only learned of her existence a few years ago. Since then they'd developed a solid relationship, made awkward only by the fact that Avery had briefly joined the ranks of women who tried and failed to make an honest man of Bones.

Avery's apartment was painted in bright tropical colors and boasted an open floor plan and lots of windows. After years in the great white north, she'd taken to the beach life and aesthetic with a vengeance. She did not, however, have the same commitment to neatness. Books and papers lay on every table and countertop, discarded clothing and shoes lay here and there, and there appeared to be no organizational system whatsoever to her collection of DVDs.

"You've got that disapproving look in your eyes, mister ex-military," Avery said. "What can I say? I'm comfortable in clutter."

"Is that what you call this?" Maddock cast a meaningful glance at a lacy bra hanging from a ficus tree.

"Oh, crap. Sorry." Avery snatched the offending undergarment and hid it behind her back. "I had a friend over last night, and things got interesting." Her fair features turned a delicate shade of crimson. "Didn't have time to clean up before work, and I only got home a little while ago."

"No judgment here," Maddock said. "Last night, Bones talked me into bar-hopping in Panama City with a couple of girls who were barely old enough to drink."

Avery quirked an eyebrow. "Finally on the rebound?"

"No, just humoring Bones."

"So her bra didn't end up dangling from a lampshade?"

Maddock's cheeks heated. "Were you able to find that research I needed?"

"Fine, change the subject. Like I told you I've only been home from work for a few minutes. Do you really think Tam would let me take a day off to sort through reams of Dad's pirate research?"

Tam Broderick headed up the Myrmidon Squad, of which Avery was a member. She was a faithful ally but also a demanding leader who never forgot a debt owed.

"Even a Myrmidon is allowed to take a personal day every now and then."

Avery laughed. "I don't get enough days off to blow them on one of your treasure hunts."

"Yeah, but this one is a pirate treasure. You can't deny that's your bailiwick."

"Don't try to tempt me, Maddock. I've got plenty on my plate at the moment. Come on. I've got the stuff laid out. If Dad had anything on Black Caesar, it should be among this stuff."

Hunter Maddock, Dane and Avery's father, had devoted his life to researching pirates and pirate treasure. Although his specialty was Captain Kidd, he'd done extensive research on many of the buccaneers that plied the seas during the Golden Age of Piracy. Much of the information he'd collected was anecdotal, and could not be found in books or online. It was this research that covered the kitchen table and counters.

"See? It's not all my mess," Avery said, correctly reading his mind.

Avery put a frozen pizza in the oven, then poured two frosty mugs of Moosehead lager, calling Maddock a "Philistine" when he said he'd be happy to drink from the bottle. "No wisecracks about Canadian beer," she warned.

"I'm saying nothing." Though he was loathe to admit it, Maddock enjoyed the full flavor, light malt base, and crisp finish of the Canadian brew. He took a swallow and nodded approvingly. "Not bad."

They set to sorting through Hunter Maddock's research. It took all of Maddock's self-control not to suggest an organizational system. Though highly competent in her professional research, Avery was much more relaxed about her personal life, and these papers, the only thing of their father's that had been passed along to her, were firmly planted in that realm.

After twenty minutes of searching, Avery let out an "Aha!" and held up a few sheets. "There's not much here, but it's all on Black Caesar."

They cleared space at the table, and Avery read the highlights of the papers around mouthfuls of Margherita pizza. The first page was a biographical sketch, the details of which were already familiar to Maddock. It was the second page where things got interesting.

"Listen to this," Avery said. "Black Caesar reportedly had the ability to conjure a thick fog that would blind his enemies. He often used this as a means of escape when the odds weren't in his favor. He's got notes from all sorts of different sources repeating the same story." She paused to wipe a bit of tomato sauce off of the page.

"You're spraying food. Would it kill you to swallow before you speak?"

Avery rolled her eyes. "If Bones were here, can you imagine the pun he'd make out of that statement?"

"The fact that your mind went there too says a lot about you."

"I used to teach at the university level. The kids rubbed off on me."

"Of course they did." Maddock scooted his chair closer to his sister. "Anything about how, exactly, he created the fog? Dad used the word 'conjure,' and he always chose his words with care."

"I don't know," Avery began, moving to the second page. "Maybe the same way he made ghosts appear?"

Maddock frowned. "Ghosts?"

"Ghosts. Spirits. Genies. Each account uses a different term, but all the people Dad talked to agreed that Caesar had a way of calling mystical spirits to his aid."

"So he was some sort of wizard with spirits and fog to do his bidding?"

"Seems like it. At least, that's what the legends say." Avery took a drink and stared out the sliding glass door toward the distant waters of the Gulf of Mexico, just visible from her apartment. "There must be something to the legend, or else Dad wouldn't have recorded these accounts. He was judicious about what information he kept and what he discarded."

"I didn't know that." Maddock and his father had enjoyed a close relationship, but they'd mostly stuck to traditional father and son activities. While Hunter had often regaled him with tales of the sea, he'd reserved the serious discussion of pirate research for his time with Avery. Even now, the revelation that his father led a secret life still stung, and Maddock couldn't deny that he felt a touch of jealousy that a part of his father's life had been reserved for Avery, but he knew he'd gotten the best parts of his father and she'd been left with scraps. Any petty jealousy he felt was overwhelmed by the genuine sympathy he felt for her.

"A few years ago, I'd have chalked it up to him

finding the story interesting enough to write down, but since I met you guys," she rolled her eyes in his direction, "I can no longer dismiss the supernatural as mere legend." She let out a huff of breath. "Life was so much easier when I was an only child."

"Easy is boring."

"You low-key sounded just like Bones. It's disconcerting." Avery moved on to the next page, scanning it quickly, occasionally whispering something Maddock could just make out.

"Magic ring… controlled spirits… harem of over one hundred women… gold and treasure…"

"Is this about King Solomon?"

Avery frowned. "No, it's about Black Caesar. According to this, he had a magic ring that he brought with him from Africa. It was taken from him when the slavers captured him but he befriended a crewman and convinced the man to steal the ring back for him. It was with this ring that he called up the storm that allowed him to escape. He told only a precious few about its existence, and vowed that it would be the inheritance of the most worthy of his children. With a harem of a hundred women, I imagine there were plenty of contenders vying for the prize." She looked up from her reading. "What made you think of Solomon? The treasure and the harem?"

"That was part of it; there was more. King Solomon had a magic ring that allowed him to control demons, or genies, depending on the story. And then there's what Bones and I found inside Caesar's headquarters."

"What was that?"

He reached into his pocket and took out the memory card on which his photos of the headquarters were stored. "If you'll let me borrow your laptop, I'll show you." A few minutes later, they were staring at a high resolution of the strange seal that had been carved into the floor of Caesar's cave.

"That's King Solomon's Seal, all right." Avery brushed a stray lock of hair out of her eyes and leaned in closer. "You think it's possible that Black Caesar's magic ring was Solomon's ring?"

"This was Solomon's signet," Maddock tapped the screen. "It was engraved in his ring. How else would Caesar have known the particulars of this image?"

To his surprise, Avery didn't raise any objection. "It's the wrong time period for the Star of David. Besides, these six dots set it apart." She stood and began pacing. "Caesar was raised in Africa. Somehow, this ring falls into his hands. Maybe he knows what it is, maybe not, but he begins to tap into its power. When he turns pirate in the New World, he uses its power to his advantage. The ring is the source of his success and he adopts its symbol as his own. Carves it into his headquarters."

"As you know, I've seen far more unlikely scenarios prove to be true."

"As have I," she agreed. "Again, only since I met you. So, what do you think happened to it?"

"I'm almost certain it wasn't in his headquarters at Caesar's Spring. I don't think Nomi expected it to be there, either. She was really only interested in his journal and papers."

"Nomi's the chick that threw the grenade at you?"

"Not at me, exactly, but she definitely didn't care if she killed us."

Avery seemed not to hear. "She probably thought the journal would lead her to the hiding place. But what if he didn't hide it? What if he kept it with him until he died?"

Maddock pondered the question, slowly chewing his pizza. Black Caesar had ended his career in the service of Blackbeard, whose treasure he and Bones had discovered years before. Rather, they had confirmed the fate of the treasure, and he was confident that nothing resembling Solomon's ring had been a part of it.

"Caesar was captured, tried, and executed," he said. "Wonder what happened to his personal effects?"

"He was a pirate. Anything he owned would have been forfeit." Avery was still pacing. "But it's also true he didn't have the ring with him. Maybe he was afraid

Blackbeard would try and take it from him."

"Which he probably would have," Maddock said.

Avery nodded. "In which case he would have left it somewhere safe until he returned for it."

"Any ideas?"

"Caesar's Rock. The headquarters here in the Keys."

"It's awfully small," Maddock said doubtfully. "And I can't imagine how many people have been over it searching for artifacts."

"I know," Avery admitted. "But I think it's worth checking out. In fact, maybe I'll give it the once-over while you follow the other trail."

"Sure, send us a thousand miles away while you spend an afternoon paddling over to Caesar's Rock."

"Hey, I'm the one with a full-time job, remember?"

"All right, but I don't want you to go alone. Most likely, the island was one of the first places Nomi searched, but I'll send one of the crew just to be safe."

"Not Bones," she said quickly. "You can take him with you."

"Gee, thanks," Maddock said. "I can't wait to tell him he's missing out on a beach trip."

CHAPTER 10
Modron Castle, Cornwall

Isla descended the winding staircase into the bowels of the earth far beneath Modron castle. She'd never been invited down here before, and she supposed it was an honor to be granted access to whatever lay beneath the dungeon level.

She passed along a narrow corridor lined with cells. Rusted bars sealed off primitive-looking stone cells. Beyond lay a torture chamber equipped with racks and an iron maiden. She gave a little shiver at the sight. Modron was a replica of an ancient castle, at least on the outside. Inside, it was equipped with all sorts of modern trappings and high-tech bells and whistles. Why had the builder chosen to include a dungeon from out of the Dark Ages?

On the far end of the torture chamber, a solitary suit of armor kept silent watch over the grim scene. Feeling an irrational tremor of anxiety, she raised the visor to reveal a touchpad.

A suit of armor hiding the secret entrance. How cliché.

She pressed her hand to it and watched as a green light scanned her palm. A tremor ran from the soles of her feet, up her legs, along her spine, and up to the base of her neck. She realized, with a touch of surprise, that the floor was vibrating. Slowly, the spot on which she stood sank into the floor.

Darkness surrounded her, and she soon lost all sense of how deeply she plunged into the depths. Finally, the platform ground to a halt and a line of tiny, red lights clicked on in front of her, pointing the way down a short passageway to a closed door.

The floor was of polished concrete, the walls bare cinder blocks. There was a newness about the space that suggested it was a very recent addition. It certainly did not fit in with the rest of the Modron ambiance.

She had almost reached the door when it swung open before her and a figure cloaked in shadow stepped through. She recognized the shaved head and sturdy build of Gowan. The presence of the security guard, or whatever he was, was a sure sign that Nineve waited on the other side of the door. The man always shadowed her.

"About time," Gowan said in his slow, southeastern United States drawl. He made a show of checking his watch. "She's been pacing the floor ever since she got word of your find."

Isla swallowed her retort. She could have told him that she hadn't spared a moment, had driven as fast as she dared from Glastonbury to the castle here in Cornwall. But to do so would imply that she owed Gowan any sort of explanation. She didn't answer to him, and she wouldn't act as if she did. Instead, she merely made a one-shouldered shrug and turned sideways in order to slip past him.

Gowan caught her wrist in a powerful grip. Instinctively, she twisted and yanked her arm back, breaking his grip. "Hands off."

Surprise dawned across his broad, pale features, and he let out a huff that might have been a chuckle. No longer trying to grab her, he extended his arm at waist level and pressed it to the door frame, impeding her path.

He leaned in close. The red lights danced on the beads of sweat that rolled off his shaved scalp and shone on his blond, almost white, stubble.

"I'm on your side." His breath smelled of peppermint, but Isla found it disconcertingly sour. "Nineve's impatient. If she makes up her mind that you're late, contradicting her will only make it worse. Trust me."

Isla couldn't quite bring herself to smile, but she managed a nod. "Thank you."

Seemingly satisfied, Gowan moved to the side and let her pass. She heard the door close behind her.

"Did you stop for breakfast?" Nineve's voice asked from the darkness.

Isla wasn't sure how to respond without coming across as if she were arguing. She settled for the simple truth. "No."

"Good. I won't tolerate time-wasting. We have too much to do." She let out a long, loud breath. "Forgive me. I am not always easy to work with."

Isla didn't know if the woman was sincere but decided there was no harm in playing along. "I understand. You've met my mother."

Nineve laughed. "Perhaps that's why she and I get along so well. Follow me."

Isla moved toward the sound of the woman's voice and soon a low, arched doorway became visible, illuminated by the scant light coming from somewhere beyond. A dark form resolved into Nineve's silhouette, and Isla followed her down a short hallway. Up ahead the light grew brighter, uneven like an open flame.

They emerged in a forest clearing. No, that was impossible. Isla stopped short, looking around. The floor was soft beneath her feet, the open space dominated by the trunk of an ancient tree that rose up into the darkness. Lanterns hung from its branches, shining down on the soft grass and scattered boulders.

Nineve's face split into a gentle smile that served to enhance her striking beauty. The tall, blonde woman with her high cheekbones and ever so slightly tilted blue eyes was the sort that made other women feel insecure simply by standing nearby.

"What do you think?" Nineve asked.

"It's remarkable," Isla said truthfully. She knelt and touched the dirt path on which they trod. She realized it was the same sort of rubbery faux surface used on certain athletic fields. She ran her fingers through the grass. It, too, was artificial.

"We wanted the entryway to the temple to have a natural feel."

"You succeeded," Isla said. Now that she knew what

she was looking at, she could easily make out the walls, expertly painted and mounted with false shrubbery, vines, and branches.

"We'll eventually bring this entire level up to scratch, but the temple was the first priority. Come."

She followed Nineve along the path and up to the tree. Isla marveled at the attention to detail that had gone into crafting it. Its bark surface was rough and broken by various symbols carved into its surface. The sculptor, or whatever sort of crafter created this masterpiece, had succeeded in making everything look old. The scarred trunk spoke of centuries it had never seen. She felt the urge to run her fingers along it, prove to herself it was not the genuine article, but now was not the time to appear anything less than fully composed.

Nineve paid her no mind. She pressed several different symbols in a sequence, too fast for Isla to follow. A doorway swung back and she stepped in.

Isla followed her in. Sconces on the walls lit the circular room. A simple stone altar dominated the center of the space. The floor was covered with pagan symbols. Ten paces from the altar, low stone benches ringed the worship space, with openings at the compass points. A series of recessed areas, each a hand's breadth apart, filled the walls that surrounded the temple. Most were empty but a few held familiar items: The Spear of Lug, the Sword of Nuada, the Stone of Destiny, and the Cauldron of Dagda. All the treasures of the Tuatha de Danaan that Isla, along with Dane Maddock, Bones Bonebrake, and Grizzly Grant had discovered. The thought made her heart sink.

"As you can see, your treasures have been given a place of honor. Soon they will be put to important uses." Nineve's blue eyes took on a faraway cast.

"What are those?" Isla pointed to her left, where a sword and a spear occupied two more of the alcoves.

"Excalibur and Rhongomyniad. Recovered with only the greatest difficulty."

"Arthur's sword and spear? But they look like alien

artifacts." When Nineve kept silent, Isla continued. "Too bad you don't have Carnwennan to complete the set."

She'd thought it a lighthearted comment, but Nineve gritted her teeth.

"King Arthur's dagger is lost, along with Lapis Exillis and Arthur himself. All thanks to Dane Maddock."

Isla's heart lurched. Maddock had assured her that he and Bones had seen things she would never believe but he hadn't elaborated. They'd had far too little time together for a bond of trust to form, and then Isla had ruined it by running away in fear. She'd left Maddock a note, begging for the chance to explain, but he hadn't responded. She swallowed the lump in her throat.

"I'm not familiar with Lapis Exillis."

"It doesn't matter now. Tell me what you found in Glastonbury."

Isla described the secret passageway she'd found hidden beneath the Abbey, and all that she'd seen as she searched for the ring. She kept descriptions to a minimum, reckoning Nineve would ask her to elaborate if necessary. When she finished, Nineve stood in silence, nodding slowly like a bobblehead doll running out of steam.

"I will see to it that the place is thoroughly examined." Her face brightened. "Do you have the ring?"

A line of dialog from *The Princess Bride* flashed through her mind. "Have you da wing?" She stifled a laugh and nodded. She fished into her pocket and took out the felt bag in which she'd placed the ring. She opened it and held it out to Nineve, who reached in and plucked the ring out.

Nineve pursed her lips as she held the ring up to the light.

"It's not the right one."

"I'm sorry?" Isla couldn't believe it. "This has to be Launcelot's ring. Everything fits. I know it's Egyptian but..."

"It might be Launcelot's ring, it might even have certain powers, but it's not the ring I'm looking for."

Nineve closed her eyes and three seconds of tense silence filled the air. "This is my fault," she said, finally opening her eyes. "I have told you that I am looking for a magic ring, but I haven't told you everything."

"You don't trust me," Isla said flatly. Suddenly Nineve's temper was of no concern to her. She'd put her life at great risk to recover this ring. If the woman couldn't appreciate that, maybe they shouldn't work together.

"I *didn't* trust you. At least, not completely," Nineve admitted. "But this," she held up the ring, "proves that you are trustworthy."

"Trustworthy enough to tell me what, exactly, you're looking for?"

Nineve nodded. "Let me put this ring in a place of honor, and then I'll stand you to a cup of tea and tell you exactly what we're trying to find."

CHAPTER 11
Williamsburg, Virginia

The streets of Colonial Williamsburg were crowded with tourists, gawking at the colonial-era buildings and snapping photographs of the costumed staff members. Occasionally, someone would stop what they were doing and slowly turn to gape at Bones.

"You know what they're thinking, don't you?" Maddock asked.

"That I'm one of the tools who work here," Bones said. "The first person who asks me to put on a war bonnet and do the tomahawk chop is going to get a throat punch."

"Relax," Maddock said. "They don't mean anything by it."

"I can't relax. It's like a comic con for history nerds."

Maddock laughed. "You say that like it's a bad thing." He was a bit of a history buff, particularly when it came to Colonial America. Consequently, Colonial Williamsburg was one of his favorite tourist destinations. He'd visited a few times with his dad and once with his late wife, Melissa. Neither of his subsequent serious girlfriends had been interested, so it had been several years since he'd paid this place a visit. He was pleased to see that little had changed.

Located in the historic district of Williamsburg, Virginia, the living history museum preserved the buildings and culture of eighteenth-century Williamsburg, as well as Colonial Revival structures from the seventeenth and nineteenth century. Here, visitors could enjoy a slice of colonial life and educate themselves about the era leading up to the American Revolutionary War.

"Is there anything here for me to do?" Bones asked.

"You mean besides the four taverns?"

"Now you're talking!" Bones looked around, as if one of the aforementioned establishments were hiding somewhere nearby. "What's the chick situation?"

"Thin on the ground," Maddock replied. In fact, The College of William and Mary was located nearby, but Bones didn't need anything to distract him. They had work to do.

Off to their left, the sun shone down on the capitol building. The sturdy, brick structure was constructed in an H shape, with two large chambers connected by a central, open arcade. The steep roof of the two-and-a-half story structure was surmounted by a tall, white clock tower.

"Awesome!" Bones said.

"It is cool, isn't it?" Maddock agreed. "This is where Patrick Henry made his famous 'Give me liberty or give me death' speech. It's actually a reconstruction of the original capitol building. Some people think it's not quite accurate, but it captures the spirit."

"What are you talking about?" Bones asked. "Other side of the road, bro."

To their right, on the other side of the road, a brick sidewalk led the way to a two-story house. A covered front porch ran along its length. The sign out front read Christiana Campbell's Tavern.

"I've been there," Maddock said. "It was George Washington's favorite place to eat. Amazing crab cakes."

"What's the beer situation?"

"I don't remember. But they don't open until evening."

"Of course, they don't," Bones grumbled. "This is the lamest vacation you've ever taken me on."

Of course, they weren't on vacation, but Maddock saw no point in correcting his friend.

They rounded the corner and soon found themselves standing before the Williamsburg Public Gaol. They purchased tickets for the tour and joined the crowd queuing up in front of the sturdy, pitched roof brick structure.

"Why do they call it a gaol?" Bones asked.

"It's pronounced 'jail.' It's from a French word

derived from a Latin word that means 'cage.'" Maddock explained.

"I thought maybe it's because dudes who stay locked up together sometimes…"

"Just don't," Maddock said, holding up a hand.

"Not judging. Just wondering."

Thankfully, a costumed docent chose that moment to appear at the front door and begin the tour. Bones dropped his line of questioning and directed his attention toward the man in the tricorn hat.

"The so-called 'strong sweet prison' was constructed in 1701 and remained in use until after the Civil War," the docent began. "The original jail measured twenty by thirty feet with two cells, an exercise yard, and lodgings for the jailer. A reinforced floor prevented prisoners from digging their way out. The facility expanded over time. Most of it was destroyed during the Civil War. It was restored in 1936. In years past, thieves, debtors, political prisoners, runaway slaves, and sometimes the mentally ill were detained in this jail. During the revolution, Tories, or loyalists, along with spies, traitors, deserters, and military prisoners were confined here. Some of the more notorious prisoners who passed through these doors include Henry 'Hair Buyer' Hamilton, a British Lieutenant Governor accused of buying pioneer scalps from the Indians." Bones' shoulders bobbed in silent laughter. "And fifteen pirates who served on the crew of the legendary captain Edward Teach, also known as Blackbeard, were held here prior to execution."

Maddock and Bones exchanged knowing looks as they and the other guests followed their guide up the steps and into the gaol. The tour first took them through the jailer's living quarters. Their guide gave a little background on the gaol and the life of Peter Pelham, the jailer who lived here during the time period the living history museum replicated. Next, he led them along a lantern-lit corridor into a jail cell where he handed them off to another docent. This man, though apparently in his sixties, was sturdily built, with powerful arms and a broad chest. Maddock thought the fellow the very picture of a Colonial Era jailer.

The cell in which they stood was large and fairly comfortable, with a fireplace, pit toilet, and space to hold several inmates. Light streamed through a double-barred window, illuminating the dark wood walls and floor. This, the guide explained, was where debtors were held, usually under limited supervision. Outside, he added, were the more secure cells, which housed the more serious criminals, including Blackbeard's pirates.

Conditions in the outdoor cells were Spartan. Solid wood from floor to ceiling, heavy doors, no heat source, and only a pair of small, barred windows to admit light. Maddock winced at the thought of prisoners passing the winter months here.

"I think this is a dead end, Maddock," Bones said. "So much of this place has been reconstructed, I don't think we're going to find a ring hidden here."

"We're here for information, clues." Maddock approached the guide and asked a couple of simple questions about the construction of the facility and eventual disposition of the prisoners. Next, he broached the subject of archaeology.

"I know the site has been destroyed and reconstructed. Have there been any excavations?"

The guide nodded eagerly. "Extensive. Lots of artifacts recovered."

Maddock tensed. He knew from research that there had been digs on the site, but could not find specifics of what had been unearthed. "What sorts of things did they find?"

"What you'd expect. Leg irons, chains, broken tools, bits of crockery. Nothing remarkable, but interesting to those who are passionate about the period."

"Any jewelry?" Bones asked. "Rings, necklaces, personal effects?"

"Not that I've heard of. Those sorts of things would likely have been confiscated from the prisoner upon incarceration. As far as the living quarters are concerned, a jailer would have taken his personal effects with him when he left his post, or his family would take his effects if he died."

"What happened to the artifacts that were recovered on the site?" Maddock asked, though he held out scant hope that the ring would have been among the items uncovered.

"A few are on display in the museums on site. The rest are in storage, I assume. As I said, nothing remarkable there."

Maddock nodded thoughtfully. "You mentioned pirates. Any stories about Black Caesar?"

The guide's eyebrows shot up at the mention of the name. "You're a historian, I take it?"

"My dad was interested in pirate lore."

"Everyone asks about Blackbeard but no one asks about Black Caesar. He was an interesting character."

"What can you tell us about him?" Bones asked.

"Not much, but I know someone you can ask. Kendra Gill. She's one of our ghost tour guides."

"Ghost tours?" Bones blurted. "Seriously?"

"Williamsburg is one of the most haunted places in all of Virginia. Even the jail is haunted."

"Awesome!" Bones turned to Maddock. "Dude, you've been holding out on me."

Maddock grimaced. He'd known it was only a matter of time before Bones learned of the legends of so-called haunted Williamsburg.

"I can give you Ms. Gill's number," the guide said. "I'm sure she'd love to meet with you. She's quite passionate about her job."

"How does she know so much about Black Caesar?" Maddock asked."

When the man replied, Maddock thought he was joking, but his expression was sincere.

"She's spoken with him."

CHAPTER 12
Miami, Florida

Nomi answered the phone on the first ring. The number was private, but she knew it could only be one of a handful of people, none of whom she wished to speak to at the moment.

"Yes." She tried keeping her voice steady. Theirs was a cutthroat organization, and showing any sign of weakness could permanently harm one's standing.

"I'm in the hotel bar. Far corner table. Come down immediately."

Nomi's blood turned to ice. It was the last person from whom she wanted to hear, much less see in person. Constance.

"If you want to see me, come up to my room." Too late. Constance had ended the call as soon as she'd issued her directive. Damn! Nomi now had two choices—follow directions like an obedient dog, or ignore Constance's instructions and appear frightened. "Someday soon," she whispered.

She checked her reflection in the mirror and was satisfied with what she saw there. If Constance had arrived an hour earlier, she'd have found Nomi in her workout clothes and without a stitch of makeup. But now, she was dressed for business, but it seemed her plans for the day would have to wait. She spared a moment to conceal a tiny .380 beneath her jacket, then checked to make sure her mace and stun gun were still in her purse where she could easily reach them.

"All right, you bitch," she said as if Constance could hear her from five floors up, "let's hear what you have to say."

The hotel bar was sparsely populated at this late morning hour. A few groups of self-important men and women in cheap suits conducted business over bottles of beer and a lonely man, a pale ginger, watched a football match on the television behind the bar. An anxious frown painted his face and he held a glass of amber liquid in a white-knuckled grip.

Must have money riding on the outcome, Nomi thought. If she'd been alone and didn't have important business, she might have joined him. He was cute in a geeky sort of way. No time for that.

Across the bar, she spotted Constance. The woman could have been carved from obsidian. Everything about her was cold, hard, and dark. Her finely chiseled features only served to add to the air of a master sculptor's work come to life. Nomi hated her.

Constance pretended not to notice Nomi's approach and only looked up from her paperback novel when Nomi sat down opposite her.

"Cousin," Constance said by way of greeting.

"Cousin," Nomi replied, her cordial tone belying the tension that pervaded every muscle, every sinew.

Constance signaled to the bartender, a small gesture that somehow managed to convey both grace and economy of motion. The woman did everything, even killed, with that same gracefulness. "I ordered you a cucumber breeze. I know that's your favorite."

"Thank you."

A contemplative silence hung between them while they waited for their drinks. Their eyes remained locked on one another like prizefighters waiting to touch gloves. It was juvenile, but that was how things worked in their peculiar milieu. As if by mutual agreement they both broke off the stare when the bartender set their drinks down on the table and asked if he could get them anything else. His lascivious grin expanded the horizons of the question, but Constance dismissed him with a single flick of a finger. The corners of the man's mouth fell, and he hurried away.

Nomi took a sip of her drink. It was a bit early in the day for alcohol, but the pleasant blend of cucumber vodka and lemonade with a slice of cucumber was the perfect remedy for the Florida heat.

On the other side of the table, Constance ignored her

drink, Scotch neat. "Can we agree that the juvenile game of waiting for the other to speak first would be a waste of both our time?"

"If you say so," Nomi said, both embarrassed and slightly pleased that Constance had been the first to get down to business.

"Whatever you found in the journal, you must share it with the family."

It was a good thing Nomi had just set her glass on the table. Otherwise she might have spilled it. How had Constance already found her out?

"Nothing," she said flatly. "It's ruined."

Constance smiled, but there was no warmth there. "Come now. You don't expect me to believe that."

"If you know I found the journal, that means you either spoke with Doctor Waite, hacked his computer, or both. Which means you know the journal is ruined."

Now Constance took a drink. "You are correct, of course. But he's a red herring, isn't he? You wouldn't entrust such an important find to a man who is well known on conspiracy theory sites. You knew Waite wouldn't be able to keep such a remarkable discovery as Black Caesar's journal a secret."

Nomi felt her right hand twitch, itching to grab her pistol and end Constance for good. The woman was not only beautiful and deadly, but brilliant and resourceful as well.

"You give me too much credit," Nomi said.

"And you insult my intelligence. You are among the cleverest in the family. Deception is a habit with you. You cover your tracks even when there is no need."

"In our family there is always a need."

Constance sighed. "I am sorry you feel that way." She took a drink, frowned, and then her eyes brightened. "Let us set aside the question of the journal's contents. Tell me how you found it."

Nomi saw no harm in this. She recounted the tale of finding Caesar's headquarters, recovering the journal, and destroying the entrance. She omitted Maddock and

Bonebrake from the retelling. Those two loose ends were already tied up.

"How did you learn of the existence of this hideout?" Constance asked.

"Research. Bits and pieces here and there. Honestly, I was not confident that it actually existed, much less that I had the correct location."

"Be that as it may, you were wrong to hide the information from the family. You know that."

"Are you telling me that none of the rest of you has ever hidden anything from me?" Nomi asked, flaring up.

"Our private business dealings are always private, but when it comes to Caesar, we hide nothing." Constance's left hand disappeared from sight beneath the table. For an instant, Nomi considered reaching for her weapon, but something told her that was not what this was about. Her instincts were proved correct when Constance produced a manila envelope and slid it across the table.

"What is this?" Nomi picked up the envelope but did not open it. "My death warrant?"

"Proof that we are not keeping secrets from you. At least, I am not."

Frowning, Nomi removed the contents of the envelope—a few papers clipped together. She recognized digital scans of portions of the journal.

"Your Professor Waite missed a few things. Here and there, legible bits of handwriting survived. In most cases only a letter or two, but my people managed to sift a few nuggets from the dross. Phrases, mostly. It's the last sheet."

Nomi riffled to the back sheet and scanned it. It was just as Constance described. The ring was mentioned, though no details were provided.

"This is the only new information we have about Caesar, and we are giving it to you. As you can see, there are mentions of the ring, his legacy, birthright, and his island. Piece them together and I think that is where we should look next."

"That island has been searched before. I don't think…" Nomi froze, the full impact of Constance's words hitting her like a sledgehammer. "Wait. *We?*"

Constance smiled and nodded slowly. "Uncle no longer trusts you, but you're far too valuable to kill."

It was all Nomi could do not to faint. Uncle had sent her? In that case, she had no choice but to cooperate.

Constance nodded, seeing her discomfort. "It is his wish that, at least for the time being, you and I will work as partners."

CHAPTER 13
Colonial Williamsburg

"Well, that settles that," Bones said as they exited the museum and headed back out onto the streets of Colonial Williamsburg. "The museums are useless."

Maddock grimaced. They'd visited all the museums that had within their collections any artifacts excavated from the gaol site. No ring had been among the items that had been recovered. What was more, someone else had already been there asking about Black Caesar.

"The chick everyone described..." Bones began.

"It's got to be Nomi." The words were bitter on Maddock's tongue. Of course Nomi had already investigated the spot where Black Caesar had met his end.

"On the positive side, she obviously didn't find anything while she was here, or else she wouldn't have headed down to Florida to search for the headquarters."

"Agreed. I just wish they'd had more definitive information on Caesar."

"The thing about knowing the Old Testament is true makes it sound like he definitely had Solomon's Ring," Bones said.

The last curator they'd spoken to had shown them a journal entry by a minister who had visited Caesar in jail before his execution. The minister had been surprised by Caesar's eagerness to discuss scripture and to pray together. Knowing the man hailed from Africa and had spent relatively little time in America, the minister had assumed Caesar would ascribe to some primitive religion that did not look askance upon the depredations of pirates. Caesar had assured him that he knew for certain that the Bible was true. Or at least, the Old Testament. Despite his apparent reservations about the Gospels, he'd repented of his sins and permitted the minister to pray for his salvation in the name of Jesus.

"And then there was the last part where he says the

only thing he had of any value had been 'entrusted to good hands.' If he's talking about the ring, that means he gave it to someone. But who and when?"

"I think we should ask the man himself." Bones bobbed his eyebrows a few times and grinned impishly. It was an odd look for the powerfully built man.

"You can't be talking about a séance."

"Why the hell not, Maddock? Your angles have been dead ends. Worst case, it turns out to be total crap and we have a good laugh about it over a few beers afterward. It's not like we're going to fly out tonight."

Maddock searched for a reason to refuse. "All right. I guess it's fine for a lark. We might want to have a few drinks before instead of after. Otherwise it's going to be tedious."

"You know what bugs the crap out of me, Maddock?"

"Besides rednecks?" Maddock quipped.

"Rednecks don't bug me; they piss me off. Different level." Bones directed his glare at a corpulent man on the other side of the road wearing a John Deere cap and a flannel shirt that barely constrained his ample gut. "What bugs me is how often I have to remind your cynical ass of all the weird and inexplicable things we've seen. Can you really question anything supernatural?"

"Ghosts don't make sense. Who we are is purely made up of cognitive processes: we think, we feel, we respond to stimuli, we gather knowledge. 'Spirit' is just a word we use to describe the totality of a person. When the body dies, all of that stops. There's no supernatural being housed inside the flesh."

Bones heaved an exaggerated sigh. "And a cup that belonged to Christ couldn't bring people back to life. Oh, wait. We know otherwise. Do I need to go on?"

Maddock knew he wasn't going to win this one. "Fine. Do you still have Kendra Gill's number?"

"Actually, I called her earlier and set things up."

Maddock let out a groan. "Of course you did."

"It's going to be cool. We'll go on one of her ghost

tours and then dinner. You know what the best part is?"

Maddock knew the answer but he gave a slow shake of his head.

"She sounds hot."

Maddock couldn't deny that Kendra Gill was, in fact, strikingly beautiful. She was tall, a lithe woman in her late twenties. She wore her chestnut hair tied back in a simple ponytail, emphasizing her creamy complexion and big brown eyes. They found her on the sidewalk in front of Williamsburg's famous Wren Building, chatting with a pair of tourists, but she looked up and smiled as Maddock and Bones approached.

"You must be Bones," she said to Maddock, shaking his hand. "After all, you said you'd be the handsomest man I'd see all day."

"Actually, I'm Maddock," he said over Bone's mumbled, "Oh, come *on*."

"So tall, dark, and grouchy over here is Bones?" Kendra shook Bones' hand. "Don't feel bad. You're the second-handsomest of the day."

"What's that you always say?" Maddock asked his friend. "Second place is first loser?"

Bones glowered at him. "And what's that you were saying about ghosts?" he countered. "Something about them not making sense?"

"That's absolutely true," Kendra said. "The spirit world doesn't make much sense, but that doesn't mean it's not real."

"Don't tell Maddock that."

"All right. I'm sorry I stirred things up," Kendra said. "You're both very handsome boys," she said in a perfect imitation of an indulgent mother. "Tour's about to start. Follow me."

Maddock and Bones exchanged glances as they followed along behind her.

"You know what they say. Blonds have more fun."

"Screw you, Maddock."

Kendra took a moment to gather the tourists and

collect their tickets. As the sun set behind the trees, she began the tour. She opened with a brief overview of the ghosts of Williamsburg. The Wren Building, which stood behind her, was considered one of the most haunted. It had served as a Revolutionary War hospital, had seen three major fires, and housed on its bottom floor the crypts of several important figures from Virginia's history.

They moved along to the George Wythe house, where footsteps could be heard on the empty stairwell and the spirit of its namesake returned every year on the anniversary of his death to press an icy hand to visitors' foreheads. Next they moved along to the Peyton Randolph House, haunted by the ghost of a Civil War soldier. As they continued on, Kendra pointed out sites of interest and shared anecdotes about sightings made by visitors and employees.

When they reached Gallows Road, so named for the iron gibbets that had once stood on this lane, Kendra segued into the story of Blackbeard's final days, and the capture, trial, and execution of his crew. She mentioned two pirates by name: Caesar and a pirate named Israel Hands, who had received a last-minute, and most unexpected, royal pardon on the eve of his execution.

She next guided them along Hangman's Lane, ending up at the gaol. The gaol, she explained, was a prime site for paranormal activity, due to the suffering and death that had taken place on this site. Up ahead, just outside the oldest part of the cell, stood a small group of people carrying flashlights.

"There's actually a paranormal investigation going on right now," Kendra said, lowering her voice. "We can observe them for a little while if everyone's interested."

"Hell, yes," Bones said.

A few in the tour group glanced nervously at the gaol but most bobbed their heads eagerly. Cautioning them to remain silent, Kendra led them to a spot twenty paces away from the investigative team.

As they watched one investigator placed what

Maddock assumed was a recording device on the sidewalk a few feet from the door to the jail. Another investigator placed two small flashlights, one with a blue filter over the lens, the other red, on the step in front of the door. After extending an invitation to any spirits that might be present, a short blond woman, who seemed to be the lead investigator, began posing questions.

"If someone is with us, please turn the blue flashlight off."

Nothing.

She repeated the question and a wave of surprised whispers rippled through the tour group as the blue flashlight flickered.

"If you were a prisoner in the gaol, please turn the blue flashlight off."

A long pause and then another flicker. The woman to Maddock's left gasped.

"What do you think of that, Maddock?" Bones asked quietly.

"I think she chose the flashlight with dirty terminals or a weak battery."

He'd spoken much too softly for the investigator to hear, but she seemed to share Maddock's train of thought.

"If you were a pirate, please turn the red flashlight off."

Nothing. She asked again before moving along. Finally, when asked if the spirit had ever killed someone, the red flashlight blinked.

"Guess that battery's weak, too," Maddock said.

"It hadn't flickered once before that question," Bones said.

They observed for a few more minutes and then Kendra motioned for them to resume the tour. As they headed back to where they'd started, she invited tour guests to share any experiences they'd had with the supernatural. When no one responded, Bones stepped in. He told the story of a ghost that patrolled a river crossing on the Cherokee reservation. Maddock had heard the story before, told by Bones' grandfather, but Bones told the story as if he'd seen the ghost. His story broke the ice, and Kendra flashed him a grateful smile as other tourists shared their own ghost tales.

By the time the tour ended, Maddock thought he'd heard enough accounts of bumps in the night, strange chills, and orbs in photographs to last a lifetime. It was only with effort that he managed a smile and a few words of support when Kendra asked him what he thought of the tour.

Bones had reserved a table at Christiana Campbell's Tavern, and Kendra spent the short walk there trying to convince them that she wasn't an eccentric or worse. She'd begun working part-time in Colonial Williamsburg while pursuing a degree in American Studies at William and Mary. Her love of folklore and interest in the paranormal had led her to the Ghost Tours.

"I know I could do more with my degree, but I love what I do and I don't really need the money. My grandmother left me a small house in town and the income from her investments is enough for me to lead a simple life, which is all I want. At least for now," she finished as they took their seats in the tavern.

"I'm into the paranormal, too," Bones said. "Maddock's a skeptic at heart but he's more open-minded than he lets on."

"Fair enough." Kendra bit her lip, looked down for a moment. Her next words came out in a rush. "I'd love to solve mysteries, have adventures. Maybe have a television show like Jo Slater. Ever heard of her?"

Bones covered a small cough and nodded.

"We've seen her show," Maddock said.

They placed their orders and while they waited for their meals, it was Bones' and Maddock's turn to share their stories. They talked about their time in the SEALs and discussed their treasure hunting partnership, omitting, of course, their more sensational experiences.

"That sounds so cool," Kendra said. "I guess that's

why you're interested in Black Caesar."

"That's right," Maddock said. "My father was a scholar of pirate lore and was particularly interested in Caesar."

Kendra leaned in and lowered her voice. "If you're looking for Blackbeard's treasure, you might want to look elsewhere. The word on the conspiracy boards is that it was found several years back and the government covered it up."

Now it was Maddock's turn to suppress a cough, though the fact he'd been taking a drink at the time made it difficult.

"You all right?" Kendra laid a hand on his forearm.

"Fine," he croaked, dabbing his watering eyes with his napkin. "Just went down the wrong way."

"That's what she said," Bones blurted.

Kendra tilted her head. "I did?"

"It's a quote from a...never mind. What can you tell us about Caesar."

"I've brought all that I have on him. After my first contact with him, I tried to learn as much as I could about his life so that I'd have more questions to ask him during subsequent sessions. It's not a great deal of information, but here it is. I've also included transcripts of our conversations, if you can call them that." She took a sheaf of papers from her drawstring bag and handed them to Maddock. He handed half of them to Bones and they reviewed them while they ate.

Maddock's crab cakes were a little short on meat, but delicate and flavorful, and served in generous portions. Bones opted for the fried chicken, and proclaimed it, "pretty damn good for white people food." The highlight, in Maddock's mind, was the sweet potato muffins, which were light with just the right amount of sweetness.

Kendra's papers were a letdown. The information she'd gathered was nothing new, and even if Maddock believed that her transcripts were the records of actual conversations with Black Caesar, there was nothing there to point them to the resting place of the pirate's ring.

Nevertheless, the food, drinks, ambiance, and the company of an attractive woman lightened his mood. Even Bones seemed to have gotten over his disappointment that Kendra hadn't fallen head-over-heels for him. Over after-dinner cocktails, the three laughed and swapped stories of unexplained phenomena.

"I think I've found a couple of kindred spirits, here," Kendra said. Under the table, Maddock felt her hand rest on his knee. He flashed a furtive smile but didn't move away.

"We love all this mystery crap," Bones said. "But right now, I'm feeling a close connection to that serving girl over there." He winked at a buxom redhead who smiled back at him.

"That's Sandra," Kendra said. "I'd introduce you, but there's no need."

"She got a boyfriend or something?" Bones asked.

"No, she's just…how should I say this? She doesn't allow our culture's prevailing attitudes toward sex to inhibit her in any way."

"I'm in love. You got the check, Maddock?" Before Maddock could answer, Bones stood and made his way over to where the costumed serving girl waited.

"I think they're meant for each other, at least for a few hours," Kendra said, watching as Bones and Sandra left the tavern together.

"That's about as long as Bones can keep a relationship going," Maddock said, laughing.

A contemplative silence fell between them. Kendra gazed at Maddock as if she were waiting for him to speak. He suddenly found himself very aware of his mouth. Why did it feel so dry all of a sudden? He reached for his glass but found it empty. He felt Kendra remove her hand. What was wrong with him? Why couldn't he think of anything to say?

"You haven't said much about my research," Kendra said. "I guess it wasn't helpful?"

"No, I mean, yes. It was informative." Did his voice always sound like that? "It's just that we're looking for something specific that belonged to Caesar."

"Like what?" She smiled. "If it's some big secret, I promise not to tell. I'm a good girl...when I need to be." The smile she gave him made him feel hot all over. Couldn't their server have at least filled his water glass?

"It's a ring," he managed. "A very old ring."

"Must be valuable." She rested her chin in her hand and leaned closer. The twinkle in her eye said she knew exactly the effect she was having on him, and she was enjoying every minute of it.

"It's valuable for its historical significance."

"I love history." Kendra ran a single, lacquered fingernail along his forearm.

Myriad thoughts ran through Maddock's head in that instant. His recent breakup with Angel. Isla's betrayal. Memories of his late wife. His ex-girlfriend Jade telling him he was too selfish to ever have a lasting relationship.

But one voice drowned them all out. It was that of Bones.

Maddock, sometimes you think too much.

He leaned in and planted a firm kiss on Kendra's lips. He felt her respond, heard a soft sigh. He gently broke the kiss and they sat there, nose to nose, smiling.

"Took you long enough." She sounded a bit out of breath.

"I'm worth the wait." *What the hell? Now I'm even talking like Bones.*

"That remains to be seen. But first things first."

"Like what?" he asked.

"First, pay the check. Then we're going to have a talk with Caesar."

CHAPTER 14
Modron Castle

Isla let out a long, slow breath, stood, and kneaded the stiff muscles of her lower back. She'd spent far too much time sitting in one place. She'd love to get out and stretch her legs, but there were things lurking the grounds of Modron that gave her pause, despite Nineve's assurance that only the forest behind the castle was dangerous.

"I've got to get out of here," she said aloud. "Even if only for an hour." She'd always been the restless sort. That was why travel writing appealed to her. She loved seeing new places, meeting new people. And recent events had stoked within her a hunger for adventure of the more dangerous sort. It was difficult to believe she had changed so much in such a short period of time. But could she say she had truly changed when she was afraid to even walk out the back door? "Bugger that. I'm going."

She made her way to the back exit on the main floor. A quick retinal scan and the door swung open. Darkness and cold night air enveloped her. What time was it? A quick glance at her watch told her it was one o'clock in the morning. She'd missed dinner, but her stomach hadn't complained.

Behind the castle, a manicured lawn gently sloped down to the dense forest. A crescent moon sprinkled a dusting of silver light on the path before her. She followed it down to a wrought iron fence. Several meters beyond stood a series of tall, narrow posts; their silver surfaces seemed to glow, and they emitted a low hum.

Isla rested her arms on the top of the wrought iron fence and gazed into pitch black forest. She could see nothing more than a few meters in, but she occasionally caught the sound of a reptilian hiss, or something heavy lurching through the trees.

"I wouldn't go beyond the gate if I were you."

She snapped her head around and saw Gowan

walking across the lawn toward her. His easy gait and relaxed posture looked like that of a man out on an evening stroll.

"I hadn't planned on it." She turned away from him and returned to staring into the forest.

To her chagrin, he didn't keep walking, but instead joined her.

"The posts aren't electrified or anything," he said, "but they emit waves at a frequency that the creatures can't stand. It keeps them away from the edges of the forest."

"I wondered about that," she admitted. "Could be bad for all concerned if they ever got out."

"They won't attack unless given a specific signal, and another signal stops them in their tracks. Nineve demonstrated for my benefit. It's remarkable, really."

"Then why shouldn't I pass beyond the fence?"

Gowan let out a small laugh. "Because, when it comes right down to it, they're still animals, and no training is one hundred percent perfect. Also, some of them are quite large, and could injure you without intending to."

"Understood. So, why aren't you guarding Nineve?"

"I'm not actually her guard. I just work closely with her." He reached into an inside pocket of his jacket and took out a tin of mints. "Care for one?" Isla shook her head. "Suit yourself." He shook a couple into his palm and popped them into his mouth. "I love coffee but I have a deep, abiding fear of coffee breath. Hence the mints, all day long."

There was something so ordinary, so normal about the comment that Isla couldn't help but smile.

"How goes the research?"

Isla didn't flinch. So that was his game. Trying to find out what task Nineve had set her to.

"Slowly."

Gowan nodded. "I wouldn't worry too much about it. The bloody ring has gone undiscovered for what? Three thousand years?"

Isla kept her silence. So he knew there was a ring involved. Of course, that didn't mean he knew which ring.

"King Solomon," he sighed. "Had more gold and women than he had sense."

So he did know. "I thought he was supposed to be the wisest of all the kings of Israel."

In the scant light she saw Gowan roll his eyes. "Based on what? The 'cut the baby in half' story? Seriously, who would be dumb enough to fall for that? The man was blessed by God, granted power and wealth, but he suffered from the same disease as his father, King David."

"What was that?"

"He loved woman way too much. His pagan wives found him easy to manipulate."

Isla closed her eyes, thinking. "Hold on. But, we're pagan."

"Sure we are. That doesn't mean Solomon wasn't real...or that he didn't get played." He took a moment to pop another mint. "If we didn't believe he was real, we wouldn't be searching for his mines, would we?"

"I thought I was the only dog Nineve had set to hunting." Something high in a nearby tree let out a low hiss and a bulky shape sailed down into the darkness. She suppressed a shudder at the sight.

"You're the only dog she's set to sniffing out this particular trail, but she's had me taking a look at it as well."

"Why?" Isla tried to sound as if she didn't care, but Gowan's smirk told her she had failed.

"Once you figure out where to look, I'm to accompany you. Extra muscle, so to speak."

"I don't need any help."

Gowan shrugged. "Tell Nineve if you like. Won't do you any good, though. She doesn't change her mind. At least, not that I've ever seen."

Isla didn't bother to argue. She had a feeling he was right.

"Anyway, the ring is your deal. I've been researching the mines."

"What have you learned?"

"As you probably know, King Solomon's mines were located in a place called Ophir. The location was kept secret, but people have spent the last three millennia trying to figure out where it was."

"Any likely spots?"

"Plenty of spots. Don't know how likely any of them are." He turned away from the forest and sat down on the soft grass, his back resting against the fence. After a moment, Isla followed suit. "Ptolemy placed it in what is now Pakistan at the mouth of the Indus River. John Milton thought it was in Zimbabwe. Christopher Columbus believed it was in Haiti. Walter Raleigh thought it was in Surinam."

"I hadn't heard any of those theories. I know the Solomon Islands got their name because a Spanish explorer thought the mines were there."

"Right. Plenty of other theories. Some say they were in the Middle East, close to Israel, and they weren't gold mines, but copper."

"That would be no fun."

"No, it wouldn't at that. I don't buy it. In addition to the gold, they brought back ivory and exotic animals, like apes and peacocks. And we have a record of how long the round trip to the mine would take. All of that excludes any sites in the immediate vicinity."

"You have your own pet theory?"

Gowan shook his head. "Not at the moment. After Solomon's death, the kingdom split into Israel and Judah. Not long afterward, Jerusalem fell to the Egyptians and whatever treasures Solomon might have had were lost. I'll wager the secret was lost with the library at Alexandria, or lies buried in some dusty tomb."

Isla considered his grim outlook. Surely Nineve wouldn't set them an impossible task. "You think Nineve knows something we don't about this?"

"Always. But if it were something that might help us

find either the ring or the mines, she wouldn't hold it back. I'm sure of it."

Isla ran a hand through her hair, closed her eyes, and leaned her head back. "This seems a risky proposition to me."

"There's always danger when you go after something of such great value."

"Not to me. Risky for the organization. Think about it. One of our aims is to undo the damage done by the monolithic Middle Eastern religions. To prove the existence of Solomon's Mines, hell, to prove that Solomon himself existed, only strengthens Judaism, Christianity, and Islam."

Gowan scratched his chin, nodding thoughtfully. "You are correct, of course. I presume she wants the wealth but not the fame that would come from the discovery. The ring…I suppose she believes it has magical powers."

"I think you're right." A loud hiss, seemingly directly above them, interrupted her thoughts. "Bloody things!" Despite her reservations about the man, Isla couldn't overcome her natural curiosity. "What, exactly, are these creatures?"

Gowan seemed to consider this question for a while. "Science experiments, when it comes right down to it. A combination of genetic engineering and careful breeding. They were supposed to have all been put down when the Sisterhood fell a few years back, but loyal elements within the government worked to save as many as they could. They're actually quite friendly once you get to know them."

She whipped her head to the side to stare at Gowan. He returned her gaze for a long moment and then burst out laughing.

"I'm talking out of my ass, of course. Never gotten too close to any of them."

Isla shook her head.

"Why do you serve the Sisterhood? You're American and your accent places you firmly in the Bible Belt."

"I never fit in there," he said promptly. "I know I don't look it or sound it, but I'm fifty percent Native American. I believe in the old ways and think the world would be better off if our beliefs and traditions were strongly supported. I'm not out to eradicate the major religions, but to show people there's more than one truth, more than one way. Maybe someday I can do for my people what Nineve will do for the descendants of the Celts."

"You believe we're doing the right thing?"

He didn't hesitate. "Absolutely. There's a certainty that comes with the belief that yours is the one true God, and with that certainty comes a license to oppress, even to kill. We've witnessed it for centuries and it's getting worse. Violence between Christians and Muslims is going to tear this world apart unless we show them a different way. A better way."

Isla nodded, though she wasn't completely convinced. Gowan's was a narrow, slanted view, but it was far too late for that sort of nuanced debate. One thing he was right about—the division in society was becoming too great. Something needed to change.

Gowan yawned, stretched, and tried to put his arm around her shoulders. What an ass. They'd just had their first civil conversation and he had to go and ruin it.

She stood and forced a yawn.

"I think I'm ready to turn in," she said. "I'll need my rest if I'm going to find a ring that's been lost for three thousand years."

CHAPTER 15
Colonial Williamsburg

Dark clouds blanketed the night sky as Maddock and Kendra strolled along what had once been the Gallows Road, where convicted criminals were hanged. Maddock tried to imagine a convicted man, taking his final steps along this thoroughfare. He pictured onlookers lining the streets, some hurling epithets, shaking fists, or spitting, but most merely staring in fascination or horror. Up ahead, the hangman waited.

"You with me?" Kendra gave his hand a squeeze. "You've been quiet for a long time."

"Sorry, sometimes I get caught up in the history of a place."

"I hear you." She leaned her head against his shoulder. "I think it's endearing. A sense of wonder is a great thing."

"Bones says it happens to him, too, but only at Hooters."

Kendra laughed. "He's…special."

"That he is, but also the best friend anyone could ask for."

Kendra guided them off the main road and onto a grassy lawn. She turned on the flashlight app on her smartphone and looked around until she located a spot where strips of fresh sod had recently been put down. "This is it," she said, opening the backpack she'd picked up at her home. She shoved a blanket into Maddock's arms. "Spread this out."

"I like it so far. Want me to put on some slow jazz?"

"Pervert," she said. "And if you've got slow jazz on your phone, I'd rather not know about it."

Maddock spread the blanket atop the sod and sat down. Kendra joined him and began removing items from her pack.

"Digital recorder," she said, placing a silver object that looked a bit like an old-time microphone on the blanket between them. "Sometimes you can actually hear what a spirit is saying, but that's exceedingly rare. Spirits tend to communicate on a wavelength outside our auditory spectrum. That's why sometimes a dog will react to the presence of a spirit while its family remains oblivious."

Maddock nodded, determined to keep his skepticism at bay and embrace the experience, even if he thought it was a bunch of crap.

"Next we have an EMP monitor." She handed him a handheld device with a large dial, a screen, and several buttons along the top. Two stubs, like small antennae, protruded from the top. "We use this for yes or no questions. Same with this flashlight." She took out a small flashlight, turned it on, and unscrewed it until the light began to flicker. She tightened it again until the beam was steady, then clicked it off.

"I wondered how that worked," Maddock said.

"The spirits can't manipulate the switch, but they can interfere with the flow of a weak electrical current. We'll switch everything on once everyone arrives."

Maddock had texted Bones, apprising him of the plan. Meanwhile, Kendra had invited two friends who were paranormal investigators, explaining that it was common practice to have three or more "true believers" in order to guarantee optimal conditions.

"I take it I don't qualify," he said.

"Not even close," Kendra said. "But I hope you'll keep an open mind about it. There are a lot of intelligent, educated people who are either believers or who haven't dismissed the possibility that spirits still exist."

Maddock nodded. "So, why this particular spot?" He patted the blanket.

"Not long ago, an archaeological dig team uncovered evidence that the old gallows was located on this exact spot. It's long been believed that they were built somewhere in this immediate vicinity, but only now are we finding supporting evidence that this was, in fact, the spot."

"So, this is probably where Caesar died?"

"Almost certainly. He and the other pirates, along with other victims, are buried somewhere along this street, but no one knows where. In any case, the place where a person died, or where they lived, is really where you want to look. Burial sites are dead zones for the spirit world, pun intended."

"Assuming I buy into all this, do you really think we have a chance of contacting Caesar?"

Kendra nodded. "I've done it before. Knowing a spirit's name makes a big difference. They are compelled to respond to you, if only briefly until they can summon the strength to resist." She looked up and her eyes brightened. "Here come my friends."

Two men approached, walking hand in hand. Kendra greeted them with hugs and introduced them to Maddock, who shook hands with each. Joel was a rail-thin man in his early thirties with a tanned, weathered face, wispy mustache, and receding brown hair. His husband, Larry, was the opposite of his partner, plump, moon-faced, with fair skin and thick strawberry blond hair that he wore in a bowl cut.

"Are you a first-timer with the paranormal?" Joel asked, sitting cross-legged on the blanket.

"You could say that," Maddock replied. "I take it you guys are veterans?"

"We've been doing this since college," Larry said. "That's how we met." He looked around. "Aren't there supposed to be more of us?"

"I'm here." Bones' voice drifted out of the darkness. A moment later, he and Sandra, the server he'd met earlier in the evening, appeared. Sandra, who had changed into street clothes, was already acquainted with Joel and Larry, and introduced them to Bones.

"This is going to rock," Bones said, rubbing his hands together. "If this works, I'm totally going to have you guys ring up Jimi Hendrix."

Joel frowned and Maddock quickly assure him that Bones was not mocking them. "He's a believer and he's always wanted to meet Hendrix." The ghost hunter shrugged and turned his attention to Kendra. "We brought the PX. Want to use it?"

"What's a PX?" Maddock asked.

"It's a device that measures certain environmental conditions and matches them up with words in its database. It's basically a Magic 8 Ball, but with several hundred possible responses."

"We disagree on that," Joel explained, "but it's Kendra's party so we'll do it the old-fashioned way." The meaningful look he directed at the digital recorder explained his meaning.

Kendra pressed her hands to her chest, miming a heart attack. "I get to be in charge!" But despite her moment of levity, she was quickly all business. She reminded everyone to turn off their cell phones. Next, she turned on the EMP monitor, adjusted the knob, and handed it to Maddock. "Keep an eye on the row of lights at the top, as well as the meter on the screen." She tapped the green digital display, where a black arrow pointed to the left. "Hold it level in your lap where everyone can see it." Next, she turned on the digital recorder and the flashlight, then nodded to Larry.

"Everyone adopt a spirit of welcoming," Larry said, "and open yourselves to the spirit world." He took out a tiny bell, and rang it three times. It produced a thin, high-pitched note, scarcely audible. Seemingly satisfied, he pocketed the bell and inclined his head toward Kendra. A thick canopy of silence drew over the six people seated in a circle.

"We invite the man called Caesar to join us," Kendra said in a firm, clear voice. As they waited, Maddock realized his heart was racing a mile a minute, his eyes locked on the device in his hands. After a minute's wait, Kendra asked, "Caesar, are you with us?"

Nothing.

She waited a few seconds. "We respectfully ask you to join us. We have questions that only you can answer."

Sandra gasped and pointed to the flashlight, which

flickered.

"Caesar, are you with us?" Kendra asked.

Maddock's jaw dropped as the arrow on his digital display swept over to the right and the first three lights on the device lit up.

"Something happened," he whispered. He suddenly felt clammy all over as if a pocket of cold, damp air had descended upon this spot.

"We saw," Joel said, his voice serene.

"If you are the man who was known to some as the pirate called Black Caesar, turn off the flashlight," Kendra said.

The flashlight flickered and the EMP monitor registered another hit.

"Wicked," Bones whispered.

Kendra proceeded with a set of questions about Caesar's life and death, all simple "yes or no" questions. The first few times she asked that Caesar turn off the flashlight if the answer was affirmative, then dropped the reminder after a few positive results. Every time the flashlight flickered, the monitor registered the result. Maddock knew it was possible that some sort of electrical interference could be causing both phenomena, but so far it had only happened immediately after a question. Not a single stray flicker of the light or result from the monitor. Finally, Kendra got down to business.

"Caesar, did you once own a special ring?"

This time the readout on the monitor was off the charts, the flashlight beam flickering strobelike.

"He has strong feelings about the ring," Larry whispered.

"Did this ring have any special powers?"

Again, a strong result. Every light on the EMP monitor lit up for a full second.

"Are we upsetting him?" Sandra asked, reaching out to take Bones' hand.

"It's more likely that this is something he's been waiting a long time to talk about. This ring must have been important to him," Joel reassured.

Kendra cast a nervous glance at Maddock. He returned what he hoped was a reassuring smile.

"Caesar, turn off the flashlight if you died with the ring in your possession."

Nothing.

"Ask about the island," Maddock whispered.

"Did you hide the ring on your island in Florida?"

Again, nothing.

"Did you give the ring to someone before you died?" Bones blurted.

Everyone jumped as the flashlight began to turn itself on and off. Maddock held the monitor at arm's length, watching the lights flash on and off.

Larry reached out and gave Joel's hand a squeeze.

"Wow. You know what this means?" Larry whispered.

"If he feels this strongly, the ring might be the reason his spirit never departed," Joel replied. "Maybe he's been waiting for someone to ask him about it."

The flashlight flickered again.

"I think he agrees with you," Kendra said. "Caesar, did one of your captors take the ring from you?"

No reply.

"Did you give the ring to one of your crew members?" Bones asked.

Once again, the flashlight went crazy.

Despite his reservations, Maddock found himself caught up in the excitement. "Did you give the ring away before you were captured?"

Nothing.

"He doesn't like you, Maddock," Bones said. "Knows you're a skeptic."

Maddock tried again. "Did you give it to one of your fellow prisoners?"

Flashing lights, sweeping arrow on the monitor.

"How about we try the PX now?" Joel asked. "Maybe he'll name the person he gave it to."

"How's he going to do that? You've got a limited number of words in that device and no proper names?"

she asked.

"Phonetics," Joel said.

"We'll stick with yes or no for now. I've got the list of captives here," Kendra said, taking a sheet of paper out of her bag. "But I can't wait to play back the audio recording."

"I'm going to try the PX anyway," Joel said. "I'll mute the audio so it doesn't interfere with your recording." He took out a small handheld device, flicked a few switches, and then pointed at Kendra.

She cleared her throat. "Caesar, did you give the ring to…" One by one, she went down the list, naming each of the pirates. None of them produced a result. Finally, she came to the last name on the list. "Did you give the ring to Israel Hands?"

This time everyone jumped. The flashlight flashed on and off over and over again. All the readings on Maddock's monitor shot up to the red and remained there. After ten seconds, the flashlight went black and the readings on the monitor flatlined. No one said a word.

Kendra put a hand on Maddock's knee and gave it a squeeze.

"Amazing," Sandra marveled.

"Caesar," Kendra said tentatively, "are you still with us?"

They waited, but whatever force or presence had been with them had gone.

"That was freaking awesome!" Bones said. "Still a skeptic, Maddock?"

Maddock shrugged. He had no explanation for what they'd just experienced.

"You'll get there." Bones turned to Joel. "What does the PX have to say?"

Joel stared slack-jawed at Bones for a full second, and then he gave a quick shake as if coming out of a trance.

"Sorry, I got so caught up in things I forgot to look. Let's see." He tapped the PX device. "Oh my God!"

"What is it?" Kendra asked.

Joel held the PX up for all to see. There on the digital display was a string of words.

IS REAL HAND IS REAL HAND IS REAL HAND

CHAPTER 16
Museum of London Docklands

Beneath gray skies, Maddock and Bones navigated the sparse crowd outside the Museum of London Docklands. Housed in a Georgian-era sugar warehouse located on the Isle of Dogs in the Canary Wharf area of London, the museum told the history of the River Thames and the growth of London's Docklands. Outside the sprawling brick building, Maddock paused, letting the damp breeze from the nearby river ruffle his hair.

"Let me guess," Bones said, shrugging up his leather jacket against the unseasonably cool weather, "you're still thinking about that chick you hooked up with. Word of advice—move on. I guarantee you she already has."

Maddock couldn't help but wince. He liked Kendra, though he doubted he'd ever see her again. In any case, she wasn't what was on his mind. "That's not it. I just admire London's history. I mean, it was founded by the Romans and some of their structures are still standing almost two thousand years later. I wish we had things that old in America."

"Maddock," Bones began, "one of these days I'm going to teach you about these things called Indian mounds."

Maddock laughed. "Okay, a *few* mounds are as old as structures like London Wall, but point taken."

"Don't spoil this for me with one of your lectures," Bones said. "Just let me be right for once. Besides, don't we have an appointment?"

"That we do." Maddock checked his watch. "We ought to be right on time."

They passed a statue of a man in Colonial garb, holding a roll of paper and gazing out in the direction of the Thames.

"Robert Milligan," Bones read. "They ought to call this place Milligan's Island."

Maddock groaned, shook his head, and led the way

forward. Up ahead, a white sign marked *Museum of London Docklands* hung above the entrance. Inside, a map listed the museum's various exhibits, including the London Sugar and Slavery, Sailor Town, First Port of Empire, Warehouse of the World, and many more.

"Dude, you're not going to make me wander through all of these, are you?" Bones asked.

"We'll see. You're interested in ships and the sea, aren't you?"

"I'm interested in the chicks in bikinis who line the seashores. The rest of it I can take or leave."

They made their way quickly through the exhibits, pausing once for Bones to admire a mummified cat and rat. Maddock took in the sights as they walked. The museum was filled with artifacts related to sailing, shipping, warehousing, even whaling.

"You think the ring ended up here?" Bones said in a low voice, stealing a glance at a display devoted to the gibbets from which the corpses of pirates were hung in iron cages after their execution.

"I don't know. That's one of the things I plan on asking." Maddock looked up and flashed a friendly smile as a tall, thin man of middle years hurried to greet them.

"You must be Misters Maddock and Bonebrake," he said, shaking their hands in turn. "I recognized you by Mister Bonebrake's description. I'm Gareth Brent."

"Pleasure to meet you. I'm Dane, but most people call me Maddock. You can call him Bones."

"Very good." Gareth was only an inch or two shorter than Bones, but he looked up at him and squinted as if trying to see something at a great distance. Then he gave his head a shake and invited them to follow him to a nearby break room. He poured three cups of coffee, grimaced when Maddock and Bones said they preferred theirs black, then sat down and got to business. "How may I help you?"

"We're researching a pirate named Israel Hands," Maddock said. "I understand you're the man to whom we should speak."

Gareth's eyebrows flitted up. He ran a hand through his unkempt, sandy hair, and slowly shook his head. "I didn't realize I was considered an expert on Mister Hands."

"You're the closest thing we've been able to find," Bones said. "There's not a lot of information about him out there, and the chapter you wrote a few years back was pretty thorough."

Gareth again squinted at Bones, a small frown furrowing his brow. Bones cocked his head and Gareth hurried on. "Forgive me. I know I keep giving you odd looks, but I believe I've seen you before."

"They have cigar store Indians in England?"

Gareth shook his head, dead serious. "A Native American of your size is hard to forget. It was a few years ago, in Kensington Gardens. You proposed to a...um...woman."

Bones' cheeks turned scarlet. "That didn't work out," he said.

Maddock swallowed his laughter and took a sip of coffee. On that particular occasion, he had needed a diversion, and Bones had achieved it by proposing to their mutual friend, Kaylin Maxwell. Of course, Bones' sense of humor being what it was, he'd included in the proposal the inaccurate detail that Kaylin was transgender.

"I'm sorry to hear that," Gareth said. "For what it's worth, I thought that was very progressive of you."

"Thanks," Bones said. "A hot chick is a hot chick, you know."

"About Israel Hands," Maddock prompted.

"Oh, yes." Gareth took a drink, his overly large Adam's apple bobbing. "That particular book was the pet project of a friend of mine. He asked me to contribute a chapter about a lesser-known pirate, and I chose Israel Hands."

"What can you tell us about him?"

"Well, let's see." Gareth rubbed his hands together, warming to his tale. "Though some people only know the name Israel Hands from the character in *Treasure Island*, he is a historical figure. He was known to some as Basilica Hands, was the sailing Master on board *Queen Anne's Revenge*, Edward Teach's flagship. Teach, of course, being better known as Blackbeard."

"What was Hands like? What kind of guy was he?" Bones asked.

"We can only speculate. The fact that he was a pirate, and voluntarily served under Teach, suggests he wasn't the nicest bloke."

"But he gave evidence against Teach's friends at trial, didn't he?" Maddock asked.

"He did. Of course, that could be due to the fact that Teach once shot him in the knee for no reason other than to demonstrate his authority over the crew."

"Ouch." Bones absently rubbed his own knee.

"Indeed. Teach was actually trying to shoot another crew member but missed. When Hands asked Teach why he was trying to shoot a member of his crew, Teach said it was important that he kill one of them now and again, lest they forget who he was." Gareth grimaced. "Hands had served him faithfully up to that point. His first historical mention comes when Teach captures a ship called *Adventure* and gives Hands its command. Later, when *Queen Anne's Revenge* ran aground on a sandbar and could not be kedged…"

"Kedged?" Bones prompted.

"It's an old sailing term," Maddock said. "It means to haul a vessel using a line attached to a sea anchor or a fixed object."

"Of course you knew that." Bones rolled his eyes.

Grinning, Gareth continued with his story. "Unable to free his ship, Teach took command of *Adventure*. He took all his treasure and half of his crew, which was all *Adventure* could carry. He marooned the rest."

"Such a nice guy," Bones said.

"Afterward, Teach briefly attempted to change his ways, at least on the surface. He purchased a house in the town of Bath, North Carolina, married a local girl, and purchased a pardon from the governor. But he couldn't resist the pirate's life. Hands and the remaining crew maintained a camp on Ocracoke Island, from which they would periodically conduct raids on shipping. Teach took part in many of these, and he regularly hosted visiting pirates, such as Charles Vane and Jack Rackham on the island. On those occasions he would throw massive parties, orgies really."

Bones sat up straight. "You know, maybe I judged him too quickly."

Gareth ignored him. "At some point, Hands was shot in the knee. Accounts vary, but the most reliable says that he retired to Bath to recuperate from his wounds. But he was eventually caught up in the same pirate raids in which Teach was beheaded and his crew killed or captured. He was taken to Williamsburg to stand trial, but at the eleventh hour he agreed to testify for the state in exchange for a pardon. His testimony resulted in the convictions of a number of corrupt government officials—those who had enabled Teach over the years."

"I suppose he was the only man close enough to Teach to be able to give that kind of evidence," Maddock mused, "but why wait until the very last minute to accept it? What changed?"

Gareth shrugged. "Some say stubbornness, other say it was misplaced loyalty to Teach."

"The dude who shot him," Bone said flatly.

"I discovered one account of the incident that claims Teach knew his crew's days were numbered, and that he shot Hands so he would be forced to retire, in hopes that would save him from the hangman's noose."

Bones turned to Maddock. "Just so we're clear, if you ever want me to retire, just say so. Don't shoot me in the knee."

"Knee? I'd aim about a foot-and-a-half higher."

Bones shifted in his chair. "Dude, that's not even funny." He shot a quick glance at Gareth, who sat patiently, hands folded. "Sorry."

"It's all right. I give tours to schoolchildren, so I'm accustomed to interruptions." He stared at Bones from beneath hooded lids, then burst out laughing. "Please forgive me. The two of you were trading insults, so I thought a rejoinder of my own would not go amiss."

"It's cool," Bones said. "I get compared to a school kid every day. Maddock gets the same comparison, but only because of the size of his package."

Gareth frowned. "Package? Oh, tackle!" He laughed again. "I must admit, you two are quite the pair. But returning to the subject at hand, I think the other so-called experts are wrong about Hands. At least, in respect to his reasons for turning state's evidence." He lowered his voice to a whisper. "I believe Israel Hands experienced a powerful religious conversion while in jail. His life after he left America proves that."

"I thought he came to London and became a beggar," Maddock said.

"I believe he took a voluntary vow of poverty, like a monk. He spent his time in and around St. Paul's Cathedral. He attended worship services and spent the time in between wandering the docks, sharing his faith with the sailors he met there. At least, those who would give him the time of day."

Maddock nodded thoughtfully. Having a ring belonging to King Solomon fall into one's hands could certainly lead to a religious conversion. "Anything else you can tell us about his later life? Any family? Bequests?"

"None. He formed a strong friendship with an Anglican priest, who counseled him in spiritual matters. Hands often claimed he talked to ghosts. Likely he was haunted by the memories of those he killed during his days as a buccaneer."

"What happened to him? Do you know where his grave is?"

"No one knows for certain, but I uncovered a rumor that the priest who had befriended him arranged for him to be buried somewhere beneath the cathedral."

Maddock's heart raced. "Any idea where? Or if it's even true?"

"I can't say, but no less than Sir Haggard himself believed it was."

Maddock's breath caught in his chest. It couldn't be!

"Who did you say?"

"Sir Henry Rider Haggard. According to my research, he took quite an interest in Israel Hands. It's odd, though. He didn't write about pirates. He's best known for…"

There was no need for Gareth to finish his sentence. Maddock and Bones did it for him.

"King Solomon's Mines."

CHAPTER 17
Caesar's Rock, Florida

Caesar's Rock was a tiny island just north of the upper Florida Keys. A part of Biscayne National Park, it was located in southern Biscayne Bay in the middle of "Caesar Creek," the channel that separated Elliott Key from Old Rhodes key. It was unremarkable in every way—just a small, deserted island covered in a dense tropical forest. But to Avery, it appeared gloomy and forbidding as *Sea Foam* drew close.

"You really think we're gonna find anything here?" Willis Sanders stood at the bow, arms folded, staring in the direction of the island.

"Based on what Jimmy overheard in the bar, Nomi's organization thinks it's worth checking out."

Willis grinned down at her. "Girl, if your brother finds out what you've done, there's gonna be hell to pay."

"I have no idea what you're talking about," Avery replied, feigning innocence.

"You stole his boat and his crew, you got his pet nerd playing James Bond, and you just might be walking into some serious danger."

"That's why you're here," she said sweetly, giving his powerful arm a squeeze. "Besides, Maddock agreed I could do some investigating, provided I take some of the crew with me." Of course, Maddock had said nothing about commandeering his boat or turning crew member Corey Dean into a spy. But, he hadn't told her *not* to do those things.

"Why exactly are we doing this at night?"

"I didn't want Nomi to get here first. As soon as Jimmy overheard that conversation, he called me and I called you."

The boat slowed and Matt Barnaby's voice called out from the cabin.

"That's as close as I can get. What's our play?" The former Army Ranger filled out the final spot on

Maddock's crew.

"I guess somebody should stay with the boat?" Avery said.

"You asking or telling?" Willis laughed.

Avery made a face. "Telling. You and I go ashore. Matt remains with the boat and radios us if there's trouble."

"Cool with me," Matt said. "If you two hurry up, we can stop in Key Largo for the night."

"Man, if you sing that song…"

Willis raised his index finger in warning just as Matt belted out, "We had it all, just like Bogey and Bacall…"

Willis grimaced. "Time to get the hell out of here."

A few minutes later, they rowed ashore and dragged their dinghy up onto the beach. Avery stared at the tree line, black and forbidding.

"You got a plan?" Willis asked. "Or are we just going to wander around until the sun comes up?"

"You didn't have to come," Avery snapped.

"Girl, if you think I could let you go by yourself, you don't know your brother at all."

"Fair enough. Matter of fact, I do have a plan." She took out a flashlight and a topographical chart and pointed out a spot she had circled on the map. "This is the highest spot on the island and it's almost at the center. It would be a logical place to construct a headquarters."

Willis nodded. "Least likely to get swamped in a storm. All right, let's check it out. And stay close. My dark skin ain't easy to spot when there's no light." He grinned, winked, and strode off into the forest. Avery hurried to keep up.

They wound their way through the dense undergrowth, flashlight beams slicing through the humid air. In seemingly no time at all, they arrived at the spot Avery had marked on the map. They climbed a low rise and found themselves on a broad, level spot. The forest had swallowed this space as well. If there had ever been a headquarters here, nothing remained.

Undeterred, Avery removed an entrenching tool from her pack, opened it, and began probing the ground.

"I'd offer to help," Willis said, "but that's a Ranger's tool."

"And if Bones were here he'd make a pun out of Rangers being tools," Avery replied. "Tell me you're not going to go the same route."

"Wouldn't dream of it." Willis took out his recon knife and joined her. After a few minutes, Avery's shovel hit something solid.

"Dig over here," she said. They set to work, clearing out a space, until their lights revealed a shiny black object. Her heart leaped, but then her excitement diminished just as quickly. "It's just a rock."

"Not any rock from around here." Willis ran a hand across its surface. "This is obsidian."

Avery clapped a hand to her forehead. She should have realized. "Let's dig it up."

It took several minutes to clear enough space around the stone, which was about the size of a manhole cover. Willis worked his fingers under the edge.

"If there's a snake or a scorpion under here, I'm dropping this thing like a THOT looking for a baby daddy."

"Could you be a little cruder?"

"Sorry. Tried to channel my inner Bones and it didn't work."

"Yeah, prefer the regular you. Now, let's see if there's something under here. On three?" She counted down and Willis heaved the thick stone up on its edge, to reveal a hollowed-out compartment underneath it.

Inside, partially covered in sand, lay a carved object. Avery hastily donned a pair of cotton gloves before removing it.

"Can I set this down or do you need to keep looking?" Wills grunted.

"Oh, sorry." Avery examined the hollowed out storage compartment, running her light and her fingertips across every surface before declaring it empty.

Willis dropped the stone and the two of them stood, examining the carving.

It was clearly old and African in origin, though Avery could not speculate about the culture that had produced it. A proud bird with a tiny beak and long neck perched on a thin, curving branch, which was set atop a simple disc. Avery turned it over and gasped. A line of symbols was carved on the bottom of the disc, spiraling in toward the center.

"Where do you think it came from?" Willis whispered.

"It is from Dzimba dza mabwe," a woman's voice said from the darkness. "It translates to 'House of Stone,' but you would know it as Zimbabwe. And it belongs to us."

Willis did not hesitate, but charged toward the sound of the voice. Avery heard a sharp report of a pistol, and then the sound of hand-to-hand fighting. Before Avery could make a move, another voice rang out. This one from behind her.

"Do not move. I will shoot you." It was a woman's voice, calm and determined. Avery could tell when someone meant business, and this woman was not playing. She froze, letting her flashlight fall to the ground, and stood there nervously twisting the carving in her hands.

"What do you want?" she asked.

"As my cousin said, we want what is ours." The voice drew closer.

Avery kept squeezing the carving, wondering if she could throw it at the woman who threatened her and then escape into the darkness.

"This is a national park. Technically this carving belongs to the government."

The woman behind her laughed. "Let us not play games. I don't know for whom you work, but the fact that you came here under cover of darkness looking for a clue to Caesar's treasure tells me all I need to know."

"I don't work for anyone." Avery suddenly wished

she'd enlisted a few of her colleagues on the Myrmidon Squad to help her out tonight. She'd believed Willis and Matt would be enough. And what had happened to Matt? Had these women slipped past him, or had something worse happened?

"Your friend," the woman said, "is he one of the cousins, perhaps?"

"Cousins?"

"Never mind. Put the artifact on the ground."

Avery let the carved bird fall to the sand, wondering what had happened to Willis.

"Now, I want you to…"

"Nobody's doing anything or your friend dies." Willis' voice rang out strong from somewhere out of sight, but very close by. Avery felt her body sag with relief. "I got a knife to her throat and I'm pissed off."

"In that case, we have a problem." The woman appeared at the corner of Avery's vision, just at the edge of the light from the flashlight lying on the ground. She was tall and muscular, with dark skin and fine facial features. She wore her hair in a mass of tiny braids knotted at the back of her head. She managed to simultaneously convey a regal bearing and a viper's menace. She held a small caliber pistol trained on Avery. "I will kill this woman."

"Just let them have the carving," Avery said. "It's worthless anyway."

"Hell, no." Willis said. As her eyes adjusted to the dark, Avery could just barely make him out. He stood behind cover, his knife pressed to the throat of a woman who fit the description of Nomi.

"I see someone needs to break the tie," a new voice called out. Matt! "And I think that person is me."

The woman with the gun fired off a single shot, shattering Avery's flashlight and plunging the scene into darkness. She heard Matt fire off a shot. "Bug out!" he shouted.

Avery turned to run but someone crashed into her and she fell hard on her back. She rolled over and tried to stand but strong hands seized her by the ankle. She kicked out hard and heard a pained grunt. Her left hand closed around something solid. The entrenching tool! She pivoted and swung it with all her might. She felt the satisfying impact and heard another cry of pain and the hand released her.

She stood and ran full-tilt in the direction of their boat. All around she heard sounds of people crashing through the undergrowth. Another shot rang out behind her and she instinctively ducked. Something caught her ankle and she fell, cracking her head against a tree on the way down. She saw stars and struggled to regain her equilibrium. The sound of running feet drew closer and she managed to regain her feet and stumble forward. Like a pinball she bounced from tree to tree, sharp pain lancing through her skull. She put her hand to her head and felt sticky blood.

The footfalls closed in on her. She tried to run, but her feet wouldn't obey. *I'm not going to make it.*

And then someone seized her from behind. A big hand covered her mouth and she heard a voice whisper in her ear.

"I got you."

Willis! She almost cried with relief.

"I hit my head. Dizzy."

He hooked an arm around her waist and half-supported, half-carried her to the shore, where Matt waited with their boat. When they burst from the trees, he turned his rifle in their direction, but recognized them immediately.

"Get in. I'll cover you."

Seconds later, Avery sat slumped in the bow of the boat while Willis pushed her out into deep water. Matt waded through the water behind him, covering their escape. Thankfully, they were not being pursued. The women must have been satisfied with the artifact Avery had found. Matt and Willis clambered into the boat and began to row, driving them through the water with powerful strokes. All the while, Matt kept an eye on the island.

It was not until they were safely aboard *Sea Foam* and headed south, engines wide open, that they allowed themselves the leisure to discuss what had happened.

"How'd you know to come after us?" Willis asked as he applied a bandage to Avery's forehead.

Matt sat at the helm, piloting the craft, and spoke while keeping his eyes straight ahead.

"I was watching through the binoculars and just caught a glimpse of two people in kayaks coming in from the direction of Meigis Key. I figured they couldn't be up to any good. So, I brought Sea Foam in as close as I dared, swam the rest of the way in, and found you."

"I didn't know Rangers could swim," Willis said.

"We can do anything a SEAL can, plus some."

"Right," Willis said.

"Do you think they'll come after us?" Avery said, still groggy. She probably had a concussion. "They probably had a boat nearby. I doubt they kayaked all the way from the mainland."

"If so, they're going to have to swim to it. I made sure those kayaks are no longer seaworthy," Matt said.

"That's what I'm talking about." Willis grinned approvingly. And then his face fell. "I just wish we'd held on to that artifact. Whatever was written on the bottom must be important or else Caesar wouldn't have hidden it there. Now the other side's got it."

"I wouldn't worry too much about that," Avery said.

Willis frowned and Matt shot a quizzical glance over his shoulder.

Avery reached into her pocket and fished out the stone disc that had been the pedestal on which the bird carving was mounted. "As it turns out, some of these old carvings are quite fragile."

"Girl, you are your brother's sister," Willis said.

"Maybe, except I'm cuter." She held up the disc and examined the odd symbols through bleary eyes. "Now, we just need to get this thing deciphered."

CHAPTER 18
Miami, Florida

Nomi stared at the carving that lay on the table before her. It was a beautiful artifact, expertly crafted from a bluish stone. It seemed to emanate a sense of history. For what must have been the hundredth time she ran a finger across it, relishing the cold, smooth sensation. It was magnificent...and useless.

"You think you'll learn something through osmosis?" Constance's sardonic voice penetrated her contemplations.

Nomi forced herself to maintain a calm demeanor. She hated that Constance could slip up on her silently.

"Just admiring the craftsmanship. Dzimba dza mabwe." She spoke the name like a blessing.

"May her greatness never be forgotten," Constance intoned. She picked up the carved bird and glared at it. "What secret are you hiding?" she whispered.

Nomi laughed. "You believe interrogating a sculpture will be any more effective than osmosis?"

The corners of Constance's mouth actually twitched. "I'm willing to try anything at this point." She stood and began pacing. "Caesar left this, only this, in the hidden compartment. It is important. But why?"

Nomi kept her silence. She enjoyed watching Constance flounder.

"The obvious connection is to Great Zimbabwe. But it has been searched countless times."

Great Zimbabwe was a medieval city in southeast Zimbabwe. It had once served as the capital of the Kingdom of Zimbabwe, and had served as a royal palace. Though it had long ago fallen into ruin, many of its prominent features remained. The many gold mines in the area had made it a prime candidate for the site of Solomon's Mines and many had conducted fruitless searches. It was now a World Heritage Site, but that had not stopped Nomi and a few of the cousins from conducting a clandestine exploration of the ruined city and surrounding area. They had found nothing.

"What if the bird itself is a clue?" The question didn't seem to be directed at Nomi. Constance's gaze was fixed on the ceiling. "If this is a unique species, perhaps the mine is located in the region from which they come."

A sudden thought struck Nomi. "Let me see it, cousin."

Constance handed the carving to her. Nomi turned it over and shook her head. It was so obvious! How had she not realized?

"How does it stand?"

"What's that?" Constance asked, still deep in thought.

"What sculptor shapes a statue without a base on which to stand?" She held the bird up for emphasis. The thin branch on which it sat curved downward and came to a smooth end.

Constance understood immediately. "That bitch! She broke it off of the base!"

"Someone did at some time in the past."

"If someone else had discovered the hiding place, they would have taken the entire thing. She needed to get away from us, so she kept the bit of the carving that actually mattered." Constance clenched her fist and cocked her elbow, but before she could actually punch something, a sense of calm returned. "It's all right."

"You think so?" Nomi couldn't see anything all right about the situation. If, as she suspected, the missing piece of the sculpture held an important clue, it was now lost to them, and all they knew was a blonde white girl had taken it.

"Back on the island I managed to catch a fleeting glimpse of their boat through my binoculars. I got the name and had a cousin do some research." She took out her smartphone and tapped the screen a few times. "I'm almost certain that the boat is owned by a man named Dane Maddock who lives in Key West, Florida."

Nomi couldn't stifle her gasp.

"What is it?" Constance snapped.

"That's impossible. Maddock is dead." Her head spun, trying to make sense of this new piece of information. She thought about the woman on the island. It had been dark, but if her memory could be trusted, there was a resemblance there. The woman could have been Maddock's sister.

Constance folded her arms and slowly raised her chin until she seemed to be looking down at Nomi from a high place.

"What have you kept from me?"

Nomi struggled to regain her composure, add some strength to her words. She told Constance about meeting Maddock and Bonebrake, and how she had taken advantage of their skills to find Caesar's headquarters. "I didn't feel they were worth mentioning. I had already taken care of them."

"Did you watch them die?" Constance asked coolly.

"No." The admission was a wrench. "But I destroyed the only way out."

"The only exit you know of. If you want a man dead, kill him." Shaking her head, Constance moved to the window, rested her palms on the sill, and stared out at the balmy day. "We have to consider the possibility that this Maddock person is alive."

"He wasn't on the island," Nomi said.

"Unless he was the man shooting at us from the shadows." Constance turned back around, her brown eyes boring into Nomi. "I want to know everything you've hidden from me. Right now."

"There's nothing else." Nomi waved off Constance's protests. "Understand, I've been working on this for some time. It's possible there might be something minor I haven't mentioned, but I'm not intentionally keeping any secrets."

Constance pursed her lips, disbelief evident in her gaze, but she didn't argue.

"It's possible that Maddock and Bonebrake are, in fact, dead. If the people operating the boat were friends of his, he might have spoken with one of them the night before our dive."

"Which would explain why they were on Caesar's trail." Constance nodded. "Regardless of whether or not they live, our next step is clear. We will go to Key West and find the woman who stole the artifact."

CHAPTER 19
St. Paul's Cathedral, London

St. Paul's Cathedral sat atop Ludgate Hill, the highest point in the city of London. Flanked by ornate spires, the dome of the English Baroque church dominated the city skyline, a familiar sight to Londoners and tourists alike. Founded in 604CE, the historic church was dedicated to the most prominent of the apostles.

"Let me guess," Bones began, "you know all kinds of boring crap about this place."

"You mean like the fact that it hosted the funerals of Winston Churchill, Margaret Thatcher, and Admiral Nelson?"

"Yeah, that kind of stuff. Save it."

"It's haunted," Maddock said with casual indifference.

Bones flashed a sharp look. "No way. You're just trying to pique my interest."

"Don't take my word for it. Google it. Or ask when we get inside."

Bones took out his smartphone and performed a quick web search. A few seconds later he let out a long, low whistle. "The ghost of a kneeling lady. I like the sound of that."

"We're on holy ground, Bones. Don't make me tell your...grandfather," he finished, lamely. He'd been about to say "sister," but that relationship seemed to be over.

Bones seemed to understand, and he played it off with a laugh. "I wonder if Avery would be impressed by your one-and-done with the ghost hunting chick?"

"I might see her again," Maddock said. "I got a text from her just last night."

"Really, what did it say? Probably something about your small package."

Maddock's face went scarlet. Not because of Bones' insult, but because he realized he hadn't even looked at the text.

"I don't remember," he said, reaching for his phone.

Bones laughed and slapped him on the back. "You didn't even read it, did you? Here." With reflexes surprisingly fast for a man of his size, Bones snatched Maddock's phone and tapped in a four-digit code.

"Don't bother," Maddock said. "The code's not your sister's birthday anymore. I changed it."

"I knew you would," Bones said. "Which means you changed it back to your dad's birthday." He held up the phone so Maddock could see that he'd successfully unlocked it. "Seriously, Maddock, you need to pay better attention to security."

"Says the guy who uses 6969 for every pin number."

"Touché." Bones frowned. "Bad news, bro. It wasn't a sext. She says somebody came asking about us not long after we left. She let slip that we're investigating Israel Hands. Unbelievable."

"She's a civilian. Probably unaccustomed to hiding things."

"She's a chick. It's in her DNA." Bones frowned. "Just got one from Avery. She went to Caesar's Rock and found an artifact with a code carved in the bottom. She's going to try to decipher it."

"Nice."

"She also says she's fine, but she did almost get killed by Nomi and some other chick."

Maddock snatched the phone away and read the text message, then fired off a hasty reply, thanking her for the discovery and encouraging her to lie low going forward. He knew it was futile. She, too, had inherited their father's stubborn streak. At least she had Maddock's crew, plus her fellow Myrmidons to watch her back. Hell, she was probably safer than him and Bones at the moment.

Although it was very early in the morning in Key West, her reply came immediately.

Don't worry about me. Take care of yourself.

He grinned and pocketed the phone. They'd arrived

at the cathedral entrance. He'd call Kendra later. For now, they had a search to conduct.

They each paid the fee for the guided tour which was about to begin. Their guide began by describing the vastness and complexity of the cathedral. "There are so many parts of the cathedral that many rooms and sections are unknown to most employees. I dare say one would have to work here for quite some time before learning most of her secrets." Given that the man appeared to be well into his seventies, Maddock wondered if he might have learned of a few out of the way places.

The interior of the cathedral was magnificent. The nave was nearly one hundred feet in height and separated from the aisles by piers with attached Corinthian pilasters. The rectangular bays were topped with domed roofs and surrounded by clerestory windows high above. Far above them, the dome was supported by eight piers. It was difficult to believe that such an incredible structure had been built using seventh-century equipment.

The tour continued, their guide pointing out many interesting details, including many important works of art, and seemingly more impressive to most of the tourists, a staircase made famous by the Harry Potter movies. He described at length the grand organ, which had more than seven thousand pipes, and had been played by both Mendelssohn and Handel. Finally, they made their way down into the crypt. This was where Maddock had hoped to discover something about the last resting place of Israel Hands, but he was disappointed. The crypt was nothing like he'd expected. Rather than a dark, dungeon-like space, it was bright and open. There was little here to suggest it served as a burial site. It even boasted a Crypt Cafe. As they navigated the crypt, their guide discussed the many luminaries who were buried here. Tombs and memorials included those of artists, scientists, musicians, even royalty stretching back to the early days of Anglo-Saxon England.

Furthermore, there were cenotaphs dedicated to the memories of those who were buried elsewhere, including William Blake, whose grave was lost after he died in obscurity; Florence Nightingale, who was buried with her parents in Hampshire; and Lawrence of Arabia, who was laid to rest in Dorset.

At the heart of the crypt stood the tomb of Admiral Horatio Nelson, who died in the Battle of Trafalgar in 1805. He was laid to rest in a coffin made from the timber of *L'Orient*, a French ship he had defeated in the Battle of the Nile. His black marble sarcophagus had originally been made for a Cardinal Wolsey, who fell from favor during the reign of King Henry VIII.

Though he found everything interesting, Maddock kept an eye out for any indicator of a secret burial site, a hidden door, anything that might lead to the remains of Israel Hands. Nothing caught his eye. At the end of the tour, he approached their guide.

"Are there any paupers buried on this site?"

The guide scratched his bulbous nose, frowned, and shook his head. "Afraid not."

"Any secret burial chambers. Maybe some that aren't safe for tourists to visit?"

Again the guide shook his head. "Sorry, but no."

Bones let out an impatient huff of breath. "Look, dude, my friend's not exactly a people person. Here's the deal—we research myths and legends for a television show. Ever heard of Joanna Slater?"

The guide shrugged. "No, afraid not." But the mention of television had changed his demeanor. His eyes brightened and his thin lips curved into an insinuation of a smile.

"Anyway," Bones continued, "can you tell us who knows the most about this place? You know, the secret stuff—the stuff a tourist would never see. Things that don't show up on photo galleries or YouTube videos."

"I would have to say that would be me," the man said. "I've worked here for more than twenty years."

"Sweet." Bones took out his money clip and began

peeling off twenty pound notes. "How much for a private tour? Show us all the cool stuff. If we think the viewers will like it, we'll pass it along to the producers." The guide hesitated, eyeing the money as Bones peeled off a fourth note. "Nothing sketchy," Bones assured. "Nobody's office, nothing like that. Just the interesting places. For a hundred?" He held out five twenty pound notes.

The guide grimaced, then accepted the money, tucking it into his pocket. "Very well. It's not against the rules and I have my lunch break next. Where shall we start?"

"Down here if there's anything you can show us," Maddock said.

"Alas, you've seen everything on this level, but I can show you some fascinating sights upstairs. Let us go." As they ascended from the crypt, the guide, whose name was Timothy, began listing the various rooms he'd stumbled across which were apparently unfamiliar to most of his colleagues. Most were simply small, empty spaces that had served no use for a long time. Maddock doubted any of them would be of interest, but he was determined to earn the man's trust, so he listened politely.

Timothy guided them to a place high above the cathedral and took them out onto a roof. Far below them, London swept out into the distance.

"Dude, you can see for miles from up here," Bones said. "We should ride the London Eye later." He pointed to the giant Ferris wheel in the hazy distance. "Kidding," he said to Timothy, who was frowning in disapproval. "That thing screws up the skyline." Timothy's grin vanished and he began pointing out different sites in the distance. Bones looked at Maddock and winked.

"Well played," Maddock said quietly.

Next, Timothy showed them the vast swathes of black on sections of the wall, caused by acid rain due to the polluted air of London. The problems stemmed mostly from coal smoke up until the late twentieth century. Maddock nodded along, trying not to show impatience. He sensed they hadn't yet reached a level of comfort at which they could broach the subject of Israel Hands. He asked a few questions, made conversation, showed interest in everything Timothy showed them until, finally, the guide's lunch hour was drawing to an end.

They stood in a secret room above the choir. Timothy jokingly urged them not to feel nervous knowing that only a centuries-old, nine-inch thick stone floor lay between them and a fall to certain death. Maddock and Bones laughed along.

"I should probably move," Bones said. "I weigh more than you two put together."

"I hope this has been helpful," Timothy said. "Perhaps there's something here that will interest your producers."

"Absolutely," Maddock said. "I do have a question about a story we were asked to follow up on. It's about a man named Israel Hands." He recounted the story they'd been told at the Docklands Museum. Timothy listened and nodded along, scratching his chin thoughtfully.

"I don't know that particular story. In fact, the only story I know about a man named Israel is quite far-fetched, but it might actually be of interest to your viewing audience."

"What's that?" Maddock asked.

"It's absurd, really, but there have been many accounts of," he paused and cleared his throat, "of ghosts haunting the grounds of the cathedral. Superstition, of course, but there is one story that stands out."

"What story would that be?" Maddock asked.

"Most the accounts of ghosts are the usual claptrap: a whistling clergyman, a kneeling worshiper, the sorts of things you always hear about in old cathedrals. They are lighthearted, amusing tales that add color to the history of the church. No one takes them seriously. There is, however, another ghost, the ghost of a man who calls himself Israel, which is so frightening, so real, according to those who have seen him that it gives them the chills to even talk about him. We don't share that story with the public."

"What can you tell us about him?" Bones said.

"A gaunt man, he paces back and forth, never covering more than a few meters, as if he is confined to a cell." Maddock raised an eyebrow but didn't interrupt. "He mutters about the people he killed, about atoning for his sins, about the secrets he hides, and the spirits that torment him. And he always talks about wanting to teach, as if he has a lesson to share."

A smile creased Bones' face at the mention of the word "teach." He was obviously thinking the same thing as Maddock. The ghost could be talking about Edward Teach.

"What else can you tell us?" Maddock asked. "Anything at all."

Timothy's face went ashen and he wobbled.

"You okay?" Bones reached out a hand to steady the old man.

"I'm quite fine. It's just that I'm one of the people who has seen Israel. I've never been a believer in ghosts, but I believe he is very real."

"If it helps, I've studied this sort of thing for a long time," Bones said, not untruthfully. "The hauntings that appear to be most real are still harmless. They're just trying to work out their own issues. Think of it as, I don't know, a patient lying on a therapist's couch."

Timothy nodded. "Quite right. You asked about other details. I can tell you he wears colonial garb, and he always disappears into exactly the same spot in the wall. In fact, construction workers back in 1925 found a secret door in that exact spot."

Maddock's heart skipped a beat. "What was behind it?"

"Just an empty room. Would you like to see it?"

"Definitely," Maddock said.

"You can actually get a look at the spot from up here. Follow me." Timothy moved to the middle of the room, leaned down, and plucked a wooden peg from the floor to reveal a hole a few inches wide. "This hole looks directly down upon the Book of Remembrance, but if you look over to the left, you can see the tiny door."

Bones went first, but backed away quickly. "Holy crap, that makes me dizzy. Sorry. No disrespect."

Timothy smiled and waved the apology away. "I understand. It underscores just how high up we are...and how far we would fall should anything happen."

Maddock put his eye to the peephole and his head began to swim. Bones was right. The floor seemed impossibly far below them, the splash of colors blurred into a kaleidoscope. He blinked a few times, took a breath, and refocused. *Pretend you're looking through binoculars*, he told himself. That helped a little. His vision now steady, he scanned the area until he spotted a tiny door set in the wall. "I see it. Can we go down there and..." The words died on his lips.

"What's up, Maddock?" Bones asked.

Maddock was speechless. Far below, a beautiful woman with strawberry blonde hair wandered through the cathedral. It was someone he knew very well.

"It's Isla," he rasped. "She's here."

CHAPTER 20
St. Paul's Cathedral, London

Isla looked around at the ornate interior of St. Paul's. She'd seen plenty such cathedrals in her time as a travel writer, but this was one of the finest. The architecture was impressive, the sense of history undeniable. Still, it left her feeling empty.

"I always enjoy visiting here," Gowan said. The big man stood, hands in pockets, looking around. "I wouldn't say it brings me closer to God, for obvious reasons. But there's something about the dedication it took to build this place that inspires me."

"It's not a patch on Glasgow Cathedral," Isla said. In fact, she had no opinion on a comparison between the two, but she was still annoyed that Gowan had come along. It seemed Nineve didn't want her working alone anymore.

"I'd like to see it someday," Gowan said. "Just think of what was required to build this place—the planning, the resources, the engineering, the labor, the expense. It makes the task before us seem almost trivial, does it not?"

"I dare say mending a fractured Britain will be a far sight more challenging." She checked her watch. "Almost time."

"Time for what? You've been maddeningly circumspect about why we've come here. I am on your side, remember?"

Her eyes fell on the *Book of Remembrance*. Encased in a glazed box atop an altar, the illuminated manuscript listed the names of the 28,000 Americans, based in Britain, who lost their lives in the Second World War. *We fight a new war, now,* she told herself. *A war against hate and intolerance. We must come together. That's why I'm doing this.* She mulled over similar thoughts on a regular basis these days. They were a balm for the disquiet she felt about Nineve and her aims.

"I tell you what you need to know," she said to Gowan as she turned and headed in the direction of the library.

"You tell me nothing. I might actually be able to help you, or at least do a better job of watching your back, if I knew what we were about. Also, it might help if you and I developed even a modicum of trust between us."

"Fine. We have an appointment at the library."

"What are we looking for in there?" Gowan fell into step beside her.

"Information." At the sound of his tired sigh, she went on. "I've been looking into the life of H. Rider Haggard." Out of the corner of her eye she saw a tall, muscular man with deep umber skin snap his head around and stare in her direction. Lovely. Couldn't a woman even walk through a church without being ogled?

"The adventure writer?"

"The man who wrote *King Solomon's Mines*."

"A fiction tale."

Isla grimaced. This was precisely why she hadn't wanted to have this conversation with Gowan. "A good writer does extensive research. Haggard was no exception. My research suggests he was, in fact, an expert in Solomon lore. He didn't merely write a novel about the mines; he studied them thoroughly. And he explored angles no one else has ever mentioned, at last, not that I've uncovered."

"You're telling me you think H. Rider Haggard found Solomon's Ring?"

"I don't know, but I suspect he might lead us to the ring or to the mines."

Gowan scratched his chin. "I suppose anything is worth a try. Considering how many have sought the mines, it seems clear that an out-of-the-box approach is in order."

"I'm glad you approve." Isla winced as soon as she'd spoken. Gowan was supporting her, and there was no need for her sardonic tone. "Sorry. I'm on edge. Nineve has set us what seems like an impossible task. If the Haggard angle doesn't bear fruit, I'm fresh out of new ideas."

"Understood."

The library of Dean and Chapter was located on the triforium level behind the cathedral's southwest tower. Designed by Christopher Wren, the library's collection was almost completely destroyed in the Great Fire of London. It was later restocked during the rebuilding of St. Paul's.

The library itself was much as Isla had expected. Lots of polished dark wood, shelves overflowing with thick tomes of theology and church history, and the faint musty odor of old paper. She felt immediately at home.

The librarian was an owlish man with thick glasses and pointy tufts of white hair over his ears. He introduced himself as Vernon and fell over himself making Isla feel welcome, but kept glancing nervously in Gowan's direction. Isla wasted no time in explaining what she was looking for.

"Sir Haggard," he mused, removing his glasses and wiping his rheumy eyes. "I have heard tell that he spent a great deal of time at the cathedral and made many donations. As to time spent in the library, I fear I cannot help you."

Isla had expected as much. "I know of one book in particular which was apparently of great interest to him. Perhaps I could take a look at it?"

"Of course. What is the title?"

"The Stories of Father Febland."

Vernon frowned. "Not familiar with that one. Let me have a look." He led the way to a desk where a PC stood in the midst of a jumble of discarded volumes. He saw the bemused expression on Isla's face and winked. "You expected a card catalog system?"

"Or a monk with an ink-smudged face riffling through stacks of parchment?" Gowan jibed.

Isla resisted the urge to call him a bawbag. She didn't know if Vernon was clergy or a layperson, but it still felt wrong to curse inside a cathedral, regardless of her religious leanings.

After a few keystrokes and clicks of the mouse, Vernon's brow furrowed. "Nothing by that name. I'll try some alternate spellings of Febland." They waited as he worked, the lines in his forehead growing deeper, until finally, he pushed away from his desk. "I'm sorry, but as far as I can tell, there's never been any work in our collection with 'Father Febland' in the title."

"I don't understand." Again Isla resisted the urge to swear. "Haggard was very specific about visiting this cathedral so he could learn from those stories."

"What if it's not a book, but a person?" Gowan asked.

Isla rounded on him, ready to tell him where he could stick his suggestion, but she stopped short, gaping. Of course, that was a possibility. Had Haggard capitalized the word 'stories'? She honestly couldn't remember. If not, then Father Febland could have been a clergyman appointed to the cathedral...and Isla would be an idiot.

"Good thought," she managed.

Vernon was already tapping away. "Success!" he crowed. "Father Benjamin Febland served St. James in the early twentieth century. Let me see if I can find anything else." He worked for a few minutes. "Nothing else, I'm afraid. Not to be unkind, but it sounds as if he lived a rather unremarkable life."

Isla felt the sting of disappointment. So close. "Any idea what stories Febland might have told Haggard?"

Vernon shook his head. "None. As I said, the only thing I can find about him is that he served here. There's nothing else."

Isla nodded slowly and turned to tell Gowan they could leave. Something caught her eye. Someone had been peeking through the doorway. She'd only caught a brief glimpse of him, but that was enough. It was the same man who had taken notice earlier when she'd mentioned Haggard. There was no way he'd arrived in this out-of-the-way spot by mistake.

Gowan read her expression and frowned.

"Someone's following us," she mouthed.

He nodded. "That's very helpful," he said in a conversational tone, apparently for the benefit of the man at the door. "Is there a back way out?" he whispered to Vernon, who nodded. "You and Isla get out of here. I'll lead him away and make my own way back home." Before Isla could protest, he turned and headed for the door. "I'll check it out. I think we're on the right track. You keep digging, just to be safe."

"What is going on?" Vernon asked.

"There's no time. How do we get out of here?"

"This way." He led her deep into the library, passing row upon row of books until they all seemed to blur together in Isla's mind and she felt as if they were moving in place. "Not much farther," Vernon whispered. "But I don't see why I need to leave."

"All I can tell you is you might be in danger. If someone is following us, they'll want to know what, if anything, you told us."

"But why…" Vernon shook his head. "Haggard. King Solomon's Mines? You can't be serious. It's just a legend."

"Not to these people," Isla said.

"Who are they?"

"I don't know." Isla heard the sound of footsteps somewhere behind them. She grabbed Vernon by the arm and hauled him between two rows of shelves. His eyes bulged but he had the good sense to remain silent. She peered around the shelves, looking back in the direction from which they had come. She could just make out Vernon's desk in the distance. A man, not the same one who had been shadowing them, peered down at the computer screen. "He's looking at your computer," she whispered softly.

"Bollocks. I left my browser open. He'll know about Father Febland now."

Isla winced. The reference she'd found in Haggard's

papers was an obscure one and she doubted the clue would lead her pursuers anywhere, but still she hated losing what tiny lead she had. "Could be good news for you. They might not bother questioning you."

"Just the same, I think I'll take a short holiday. Get out of the office."

"Good idea. Now, where's the way out?"

He pointed to a far corner and they took the roundabout way, staying out of sight, until they finally ended at a bookcase.

"And this," Vernon said proudly, "is our own secret door." He tugged at the side of the case and it swung forward, revealing a narrow staircase that descended into the darkness. "It doesn't lead anywhere special; only to the car park. But that is exactly where I want to be."

Isla nodded. "Me too."

CHAPTER 21
Key West, Florida

Nomi sat in the passenger seat of Constance's rented SUV and gazed through the palm trees toward the front door of Avery Halsey's condominium. It was 8:30 in the morning, time for any normal person to leave for work. Of course, they had no idea what Avery Halsey did for a living. At least, not since she'd left her teaching position in Nova Scotia. In fact, the difficulty in learning much of anything about her was unsettling. As was the fact that both Maddock and Bonebrake seemed to have largely been scoured from the public record, save for a few details here and there. It suggested that there was more to the three than Nomi had expected.

"Perhaps she doesn't hold a normal job," Nomi said. "Works odd hours, or even telecommutes."

"We'll give her until nine," Constance said. "And then we will take steps. I will kill her if I must, but I prefer not to. Killing always adds difficulties."

"But the island…"

"The island was different. Much easier to dispose of the bodies and no security cameras to worry about. There is no telling how many we drove past on the way here."

Nomi hated when the woman made sense. "At least there appear to be no cameras in the complex, except for the front entrance. Now we only have to hope that her brother or his friends don't show up." One of the details they had managed to dig up was that Avery Halsey was Dane Maddock's half-sister. That explained how she had access to Maddock's boat and crew.

"Maddock is in London."

Nomi sat up straight. "When did you learn this?"

"Yesterday. Two of the cousins tracked them to Williamsburg, and then on to London."

"And when were you planning to tell me?"

"Whenever the information was needed or it came

up in conversation. Which is now."

"Quiet. She's coming out." It wasn't necessary to tell Constance to be quiet, but it felt good to give her an order.

They watched as Avery locked the door behind her and headed down the stairs. She was a pretty girl, if a bit on the generic side. What some young people might call a Basic Becky. Blonde hair, blue eyes, fair skin, pedestrian taste in clothing. There was nothing special about her, as far as Nomi could see.

"She's in her car," Constance said. "Go."

Nomi slipped out of the SUV and, keeping to the thick grove of trees that separated the condominium complex from the vacant lot in which they'd parked, worked her way around to the side of the building. She'd considered going to the back and climbing up to Avery's deck, but that was something better attempted under cover of darkness. Walking up the front steps and knocking on the door, in short, behaving normally, rendered on close to invisible.

She pretended to knock on Avery's door, and then looked around. The parking lot was empty, and no sound came from the neighbor's homes. Hastily she slipped on a pair of gloves, took out her lock-picking kit, and set to work.

She was inside in short order. She locked the door behind her and set the deadbolt, something Avery hadn't done. Satisfied, she looked around.

The place was a mess. Clothing, books, and unopened mail lay all around. A few dirty dishes lay in the sink and a half-empty coffee cup sat on the kitchen table next to a crumb-covered napkin.

"Slob." Nomi shook her head and then began her search.

She began with the kitchen, then worked her way through the living room, bathroom, and spare bedroom. Finally, she ended up in the master bedroom. It was, she marveled, even messier than the living area. The floor was carpeted with discarded clothing, and a stack of erotic thriller novels dominated the nightstand.

"Where would it be?" Thinking like a burglar, Nomi went directly to the back of the underwear drawer. Wrapped in a pair of lacy black panties, she found an old locket. Although it was of no use to her, she opened it out of curiosity. Inside was a black and white close-up of a woman's face. It wasn't the closed eyes, stringy hair, or slight smirk that gave Nomi a disconcerting feeling. It was the fact that she knew this image. L'Inconnue de la Seine, or "the Unknown Woman of the Seine."

In the 1880s, the body of a young woman had been pulled from the Seine River in Paris. Legend held that a pathologist at the Paris Morgue was so taken with her beauty that he had a plaster cast made of her face. In time, copies of the mask, with its eerie smile, became popular in Parisian Bohemian society. The face was even used for the head of a first aid mannequin, and was used in many CPR courses. Why the hell Avery Halsey would keep this face in a locket in her drawer was beyond Nomi. With a slight shudder, she wrapped the locket back up and replaced it in the drawer.

Her continued search proved fruitless. Apparently Avery had nothing else of value to hide. But Nomi couldn't give up. She was convinced Avery would not carry the artifact around with her, nor would she leave it in the care of another. It had to be here.

"Think. Where else do people hide their valuables?" Her eyes fell on the stack of paperbacks by the bed and she smiled. The bookshelf!

She hurried to the living area and began removing and opening all the books on the bookshelf. Inside the third book she opened, a reprint of *A General History of the Robberies and Murders of the Most Notorious Pirates* by Charles Johnson, she found what she was looking for. The middle section had been hollowed out, and inside lay a stone disc. Nomi knew immediately that she'd found what she was looking for. The bottom surface was covered in symbols, a code of some sort.

She made to replace the book, but paused. Grinning

wickedly, she slipped a five dollar bill out of her pocket and tucked it into the secret compartment.

"It's not stealing if you pay for it," she said, putting the book back on the shelf. "I only wish I could see the bitch's face when she realizes the artifact is gone."

Buoyed by her success, she veritably bounced out of the apartment, down the stairs, and back to the vacant lot. Finally, she was one up on Constance.

CHAPTER 22
St. Paul's Cathedral, London

"**The door** is just over here." Timothy pointed to the small door Maddock had seen from high above. Set low in the wall just beyond the spot where the Book of Remembrance sat in a glass case. It was round like a portal, and appeared to be scarcely wide enough for Maddock to fit into.

"You said workers uncovered this?" Maddock said. "How could it go unnoticed?"

"It was covered with a thin layer of plaster and painted over. Not sure why it was hidden."

Maddock nodded. "I guess I'll be the one to check it out." He aimed a pointed look at Bones. "Somebody's been eating too many burgers to ever fit in there."

"Maddock, if we weren't inside a church I'd tell you exactly which part of my body won't fit in that hole."

Timothy's cheeks turned a delicate shade of pink. "Goodness, the two of you pull no punches, do you?"

"Not usually." Maddock looked around. "How about the two of you screen me from view and then close the door behind me? Once I'm in, you can wander around. That way we don't draw unwanted attention." Without waiting for them to agree, he took out his Maglite, clenched it in his teeth, opened the door, and crawled inside. When the door closed behind him, he clicked on the light.

He was in a tiny passageway about three feet square. Cracked brick and crumbling mortar surrounded him on all sides. He resisted the temptation to reach up and test the ceiling. Probably best to search the area and get back out as quickly as possible.

He crawled forward, occasionally banging his knee on the hard, uneven surface. He kept his eyes peeled, scanning every inch of floor, walls, and ceiling as he moved forward. Nothing caught his eye.

He rounded a corner and crawled another ten feet to

where the passage came to a dead end. Set in the brick wall was a hinged iron square. He took out his knife and scraped away the dirt and debris that caked it until he uncovered a small latch. He slid it to the side and swung the little doorway open. Peering through, he saw that it opened into an empty fireplace inside what was obviously an office. Disappointed, he quietly closed the small door and turned around.

"There's got to be something here," he whispered. He couldn't believe he was trusting in a ghost story, but he knew in his gut there was a find to be made here. But where?

He turned his light up to the ceiling and played it back and forth, examining every inch. And then he saw it. Just short of the spot where the passageway made a hard left, a section of brick had been covered over. He remembered what Timothy had said about the hidden door. *It was covered with a thin layer of plaster.*

"Two times lucky?" he said hopefully as he began chipping away with his knife. He was rewarded immediately as his blade broke through the plaster and into an open space up above.

He turned his head away from the falling chunks of plaster, the swirling dust burning his eyes and nostrils. When the dust had cleared, he hastily cleared away an opening wide enough for him to fit his shoulders through.

The open space above was sufficient for him to stand. Directly in front of him was a stone shelf coated in dust. And on that shelf lay the skeletal remains of a man in colonial garb.

His heart raced. Could it be?

Maddock reached out and brushed aside a layer of the dust. His fingers ran across deep grooves. He leaned in for a closer look, wiping away the dust until he could see that there were words carved there. He let out a half of breath, raising the cloud of dust. When it cleared he could read the words.

ISRAEL HANDS

A REPENTANT MAN

Israel hands! Maddock had found him. His eyes drifted to the skeleton's left hand. Something was wrong. He saw it immediately. The ring finger was missing.

"Damn!" Someone had gotten here first. He gave the skeleton a thorough inspection just to be safe but to no avail. The ring, if it had ever been there, was gone. And then he noticed something else — words scratched roughly into the dark stone just next to where the hand lay. He trained his light on the spot.

A RING FOR MY BELOVED SOULMATE. MY LILLY OF THE VALLEY. HRH

"HRH. H Rider Haggard. It's got to be"

So he had been right about Haggard. The problem was, Haggard had gotten there first.

"Maddock, you won the battle but you're still losing the war." Disappointed, he made his way back to the door. He hoped there were no witnesses around, but there wasn't much he could do about that. He listened for a moment, heard no sounds, and pushed the door open an inch. No one seemed to be about. Hastily, he crawled out, stood and brushed the dust from his clothing. He froze when he felt the barrel of a pistol pressed against the back of his neck.

"Remain very still and no one will get hurt."

CHAPTER 23
The Truman Little White House, Key West

Constance followed Avery down the street from a small parking area to her destination — the Truman Little White House. Did the woman work here? Perhaps she was a tour guide or something.

Absently, Constance touched the spot at the small of her back where her pistol was hidden before following along. Florida's only presidential museum, the Harry S. Truman Little White House had served as the winter White House for America's 33rd president. Presidents Taft, Eisenhower, Kennedy, Carter and Clinton also used the house. She paid the admission fee and wandered the interior, pretending to admire the exhibits.

When she was satisfied that Avery was nowhere to be found, she sought out help from the woman at the ticket counter. She had curly gray hair, and squinted at Constance through narrowed eyes, probably a result of not wearing the glasses which hung from a chain around her neck.

"Excuse me," Constance began, "I was supposed to meet a friend here. She ought to have already arrived but I can't seem to find her. I was wondering if you might have seen her." She described Avery and gave her name.

The woman flashed an easy smile. "Yes, of course I know Ms. Halsey. She works here. I'll give her a call."

Constance opened her mouth to tell her there was no need to call Avery. The woman could simply direct her to Avery's office. But the lady was already talking into the phone. She hung up after a brief conversation, turned and smiled.

"She will be here in just a moment. Sorry to make you wait but we're fussy about security even though this is a small museum." She spread her hands as if to say, *What are you going to do?*

Constance forced an easy smile, and stood, waiting.

A few seconds later, a gruff voice said, "You are here

to see Avery Halsey?"

She knew immediately that something was wrong. She reached for her pistol but powerful hands seized her by the wrists. She drove her heel backward catching the man in the shin. He let out a grunt but his grip did not weaken. She drove her head backward, hoping to catch him across the nose, but he was ready for it, and moved aside. She only hit his shoulder.

"None of that," he said. "You might as well stop fighting. You're not going to get away."

Rage boiled inside of her. For a moment she considered kicking him again, but she immediately realized the futility of her situation. Another man, tall and lean with short brown hair stood before her. He smiled, his demeanor relaxed, but she could tell by the way he stood, the way he held his hands, that he was ready to strike at a moment's notice. The old woman who had sold her a ticket stood a few feet to the left, aiming a stun gun at her.

"Who the hell are you people?"

"My name is Greg," the tall man said. We will discuss the rest in our office." He glanced at the man who was still holding Constance and gave a small nod. She felt something cold pressed against her neck and then everything went black.

She regained consciousness to find herself handcuffed to a chair at one end of a long table. It looked to be the sort of meeting room found in any office.

To her left sat a big man with a military bearing. Greg sat on her right, and on his other side, Avery. At the far end of the table, hands folded, sat an attractive, dark-skinned woman in a business suit.

"Glad you could join us. How was your nap?" the woman asked sweetly.

Constance scowled but did not reply.

The woman made a clucking sound and shook her head.

"Manners," she chided. "We are being gracious hosts. The least you can do is have a friendly conversation with us."

"Hosts? I think the word you are looking for is 'kidnappers.'"

"Sweetie," the woman said, a dollop of the American South flavoring her words, "you assaulted a federal agent."

"I'm not your sweetie," Constance said through gritted teeth. Mentally, she kicked herself for letting the woman get under her skin. After all, it was all a game, wasn't it? "If you are government agents, then I demand you charge me or release me."

"Oh, you need not worry about that. My people are busy drumming up charges as we speak. And yes, I said exactly what I meant. What you end up actually being charged with depends on how cooperative you are."

"I'll tell you nothing," Constance said in a bored voice. She wouldn't let these people intimidate her.

"Want me to persuade her?" the big man asked.

"Don't you have a tractor pull to get to? A professional wrestling match, perhaps?"

The big man smirked.

"Not yet, Sievers. I believe she'll come around. She seems the sort to see good sense...eventually."

"It must be killing you to take orders from a sister," Constance said, still trying to get under the man's skin. But, he merely rolled his eyes. She turned her attention to the woman at the end of the table. "Do you have a name?"

"You can call me Tam."

Constance barked a laugh. "Sounds like a musical instrument slow children play so they can feel like part of the band."

Everyone around the table laughed, even Tam.

"I'm going to remember that one," Sievers said.

"The hell you will," Tam said, still laughing. Her expression suddenly grew serious. "Lord Jesus, I got to put a dollar in my cussing jar."

"Just a quarter," Avery said. "Hell is as much a place as it is a swear."

"My daddy would say that's cheating but I'm going to go with your analysis." Tam rested the palms of her hands on the table, her expression grave. "That's enough foreplay. Time to get dirty."

"Whoa," Greg said.

"I didn't cuss." She turned her attention to Constance. "Let's discuss your crimes and misdemeanors."

"First of all," Constance began, "I didn't assault any federal agent."

Avery raised her hand. "Hello? On the island?"

"That wasn't me," Constance said.

"So it was your accomplice?" Tam asked.

"Yes... I mean, I don't have an accomplice. I don't know what you're talking about."

"Shame," Tam said, inspecting her own fingernails, holding them up to the light as if looking for blemishes. "If somebody else were guilty, I mean, if you could point us in a different direction. That is to say, if we've got the wrong person..."

"Oh, you have the wrong person, but I don't know who the right person is."

"Wrong answer," Tam said, still staring at her nails.

"You are wasting my time," Constance said. "We both know you can't prove that I assaulted anyone." She turned to Avery and grinned.

"No?" Tam quirked an eyebrow. "But I've got security video of you assaulting my agent." She inclined her head toward Sievers, who nodded. "You kicked him and you tried to head-butt him. And that's just what we have on video. I have witnesses who saw you do much worse."

"I will not be railroaded," Constance said. "I have rights."

"Haven't you heard? If you are suspected of terrorism you could spend a long time in prison awaiting a trial. Without being charged."

Constance's stomach lurched. "I'm not a terrorist."

"You're a person of color from a foreign country

who has committed a crime. Under the current administration that's pretty much all it takes." Constance didn't know if Tam's scowl was for her or for the administration to which she referred. "Also, you pissed me off." She said the last three words slowly and deliberately.

"You just cost yourself another dollar," Constance said, trying and failing to sound glib. She could feel her resistance crumbling.

"Give us the room," Tam said. The others obeyed instantly. Constance couldn't help but be impressed. The woman might dress herself up like a Real Housewife of Atlanta, but she wielded authority as if it were second nature.

"You going to play good cop or bad cop?" Constance asked.

"Dealer's choice. I have a diverse skill set." Tam stood, made her way down to Constance's end of the table, and took the seat Greg had occupied. "As much as I would love to bandy words with you, I'm a busy woman. I imagine whatever criminal enterprise you're involved in occupies a lot of your time too, so let's talk like two sensible people."

Constance made a curt nod but held her tongue. She sensed a deal was in the offing.

"We both know I can send you to Guantánamo and lose the paperwork. You might get out someday, but by then I'll be retired to a Pacific island drinking mai tais while an oiled-up man in a Speedo massages my feet." She paused for a moment to smile at the thought.

"What's behind door number two?" Constance asked

"First of all, you convince me you're not a terrorist. Then you help me understand why you went after my agent. Last, you tell me who you work for or with. The more you give me, the lesser the charge. That, I promise you. If I find out you've lied or held anything back, you might as well cease to exist. That, I also promise you."

Constance flinched. Her first instinct was to punch

Tam in the face, but seeing how she was handcuffed to a heavy chair, that was not an option. And, the woman was correct. This corrupt American government could not be relied upon to mete out justice in a fair and equitable way. She took a deep breath.

"All I want is to recover what belongs to my family."

CHAPTER 24
St. Paul's Cathedral, London

Maddock froze, his eyes taking in everything at once. He was flanked by two tall, solidly built men. Both had dark skin and the same East African accent as Nomi. It was no coincidence they were here. It couldn't be.

"Make no sudden moves," the man to his left, a bald fellow wearing all black, said. "We are both armed."

"What's this all about?" Maddock was stalling for time, hoping Bones might be somewhere nearby. One armed man and he'd take his chances. With two, he'd have to get very lucky.

"Don't waste our time. Stand up slowly."

Maddock rose to his feet and stepped to the side as baldy's partner moved to block the secret door. The cathedral was nearly empty. No witnesses and certainly no one to come to his aid.

"What did you find back there?"

"Dead end," Maddock said. There wasn't much to be gained from lying; there was no hiding the collapsed ceiling and Israel Hands' makeshift vault. Still, anything that might buy him time to escape or for Bones to turn up was a positive. "Not entirely a dead end. There's a trapdoor that opens into a fireplace in an office. Nothing our television show would be interested in."

The men exchanged knowing grins. Maddock saw that each held a small caliber pistol. Easily concealed, but deadly none the less. Without warning, baldy's partner delivered a punch to Maddock's gut. He took it with barely a grunt and returned a defiant glare.

"Solid," the man said. "You must do your sit-ups."

"Your wife works me out regularly." It was a juvenile retort, something worthy of Bones, but it got a reaction. The man tensed, fist clenched. "Also, you hit like a girl. And I don't mean Ronda Rousey."

"Cleo, keep your head about you," Baldy said.

Cleo looked like he was on the verge of trying

something reckless, but he acquiesced. "As you say, Ronald."

"We know who you are, Mister Maddock," Ronald said. "Our cousin told us she had killed you and your partner, but we learned otherwise."

"How did you find me?"

"Our family has many resources at our disposal. A few of our agents had a chat with your friend, the ghost hunting girl."

"If you've hurt her…"

Ronald dismissed Maddock's concern with a flick of a finger. "She is fine. We don't kill anyone if we can help it."

"Nomi didn't get that memo." Maddock was staring into the man's eyes, but watching the partner in his peripheral vision. If the man were to come closer and lower his weapon just a little more…

"Nomi is reckless, impulsive. She is being dealt with."

"In that case, maybe you aren't as bad as I thought."

Ronald bared his teeth in a mock-grin. "We only want to reclaim our inheritance. If you cease with the interference, you will be unharmed."

"You think Solomon's Mines are your inheritance? You believe you're descended from King Solomon?"

"Not from Solomon, though we are his spiritual heirs."

"Who, then?"

"It is of no matter," Baldy snapped, all business again. "Tell me what you know about Israel Hands."

"If you talked to Kendra, then you know just about everything we know. Or at least, what we theorize. We believe the pirate Caesar gave his ring to Israel Hands, who lived out the rest of his days in London. The fact that you're here tells me you learned of the connection between Hands and the cathedral."

"And why did you go through that door?" Ronald gestured with his pistol.

Maddock shrugged. "The crypt was a dead end. The

tour guide told us about a secret door. I figured it was worth a look."

"Where is Bonebrake?"

"Wandering around, hoping his dumb luck will kick in. He tends to operate that way."

Ronald sighed, then, without taking his eyes off of Maddock, spoke to his partner.

"Cleo, see what's back there."

Cleo hesitated. "Should we dispose of him first?"

"We'll keep him for the time being. I am certain he has more information. I'll let you be the one to extract it if you like."

Cleo beamed. "Christmas is coming early this year." He gave Maddock a long stare, then, after checking to make certain no one was looking, slipped into the passageway.

"Close that door," Ronald said. "Do it slowly."

Maddock turned, squatted, and pushed the door closed. His heart was in his throat. What he was about to do was reckless, perhaps suicidal, but he'd get no better chance. He twisted like a swimmer changing directions and pushed hard off of the wall. He shot forward like a torpedo, driving into Ronald's knees and bearing him to the ground.

The pistol discharged and the side of Maddock's head burned. No time to wonder how badly he'd been wounded. He lurched forward, seized the wrist of Ronald's gun hand and forced it to the floor. Winded, Ronald could only manage a feeble punch with his free hand. It glanced off of Maddock's forehead, but he scarcely felt it. Knowing he might have only seconds before Cleo came to investigate the gunshot, he drove his fist once, twice, three times into Ronald's temple. The man went limp and Maddock tore the pistol free.

Springing to his feet, he turned to see the secret door slowly swing open. He crossed the intervening space in two steps and kicked the solid stone door with all his might. It flew backward and Cleo's muffled grunt told him he'd hit his target.

Behind him, Ronald was sitting up and shaking his head, trying to clear the cobwebs. Maddock drove a knee into his forehead as he ran past on his way to the exit.

"He tried to rob me!" Maddock shouted to a cluster of shocked-looking elderly tourists. "Somebody call the police."

He kept running, hoping he wouldn't hear the report of Cleo's pistol. *Just a little farther and I'm home free.* Behind him, someone screamed.

Isla steered the hired Nissan around the corner, keeping her eyes peeled for Gowan. She hadn't heard a peep from him since they'd separated. Their understanding was that, in situations such as these, she would take care of herself, and let him do the same. Still, she didn't feel right abandoning him. They were partners of a sort.

Up ahead, she saw a commotion among the pedestrians milling on the pavement. She hit the gas and the car lurched forward. She'd chosen it because it was a nondescript family car that would draw no undue attention, but she wished it had a bit more power.

As she drew near the front of the cathedral, she spotted the source of the disturbance. Two men stood on the steps just below the doorway, looking up and down the stretch of street in front of St. Paul's Churchyard. One man's face was a mask of blood. The other, whom she recognized as the eavesdropper from earlier, was pointing a pistol around as if he intended to shoot everyone in sight.

"Oh my God. What has happened?" Her first thought was that they must be chasing Gowan. She had to help him. The man with the pistol pointed and the two descended the steps and began to run. "They've spotted him."

A line of slow-moving vehicles slowed Isla down. Bloody London traffic. She was ahead of the two men but not by much. She pounded the steering wheel. "Move, you bawbags!" Then, with a rush of breath and a dizzying lurch of her stomach, she whipped into the oncoming lane and put the pedal to the floor.

Horns blared and a taxi cab ran up onto the opposite pavement to avoid crashing into her. Isla kept the Nissan as close to the center line as she could, squeezing past the blessedly sparse line of oncoming vehicles. All the while she kept looking for Gowan.

"Where the hell are you?"

A deep, booming blast from the horn of a tour bus reverberated in her ears and she looked up to see a mass of orange and black filling her vision. Cursing, she yanked the wheel to the left, shot through the line of traffic she'd been trying to pass. Somehow, she ended up unscathed, flying down New Change.

"Bloody hell," she breathed. She'd outdistanced the men who'd been stalking them, but had she lost Gowan?

Then she spotted a familiar figure dashing along the pavement, headed toward Paternoster Row. But it wasn't who she suspected to see.

"Maddock?" It couldn't be. But it certainly was, and a few paces ahead was Bonebrake. And if they were here, that could only mean they were looking for the same thing as she. It would be too great a coincidence for anything else to be true.

She zipped past them and skidded to a halt at the corner of New Change and Cheapside, stuck her head out the window, and shouted at the two shocked-looking men.

"Get in!"

Isla felt every muscle in her body tense as Maddock and Bones climbed into the car. Bones spread his bulk across the back seat while Maddock slid into the front passenger seat. He didn't speak or even meet her eye as they drove away. Her mind was a whirl of emotions. Why was he hunting for the mines? What was she going to say to him? Would he even talk to her considering he'd frozen her out ever since their parting in Scotland? Then again, she had just saved them from their pursuers. He owed her a thank-you, at a minimum.

"Appreciate the lift," Bones said, seemingly reading her thoughts.

"You're welcome." She turned to glare at Maddock. He stared straight ahead, but a slight reddening of his ears said he was keenly aware of her gaze.

"Thanks," he finally said.

She nodded and focused on the road. She was certain they had left the two men behind, but she kept checking her mirrors none the less.

"Any idea who those two men were?" she asked.

"I don't know anything," Bones said. "I was hanging loose outside when all of a sudden, Maddock bursts through the door and tells me to run for it."

Isla couldn't detect any emotion in Bones' voice. She knew the man disapproved of her, and was certain she hadn't forgotten the way she'd left them the last time they'd been together.

"You got any ideas, Maddock?" Bones said. "Did they say anything?"

"I'll tell you later," Maddock said in a flat tone. "You can drop us off anywhere," he added.

"Not until I've gotten you well away, just to be safe. But given that they were stalking me, too, I think it would be fair to tell me what you know. It might help keep me safe."

"Dude, you've got some nerve saying that to us after what you did," Bones said.

There it was. Isla had known it was coming, but her face still turned a crimson mask of shame. "I know how it looked," Isla began.

"Looked? Chick, we don't care about how it looked. We care about what you did. You ditched us and ran off with the people who were trying to kill us."

Isla stole a glance at Maddock, who betrayed no emotion.

"You're right. I did run away. With my mother."

"Who is a bigwig with the Tuatha de Danaan," Bones said.

"Who, until a few minutes before that, I had thought

dead." Her eyes began to mist and sadness pinched at the back of her throat. Don't cry in front of him! "Bullets were flying. I was frightened to death, and in shock at seeing my mother again. I didn't run *from* you so much as I ran *to* her." She turned to Maddock, a note of pleading in her voice. "Dane, you lost both of your parents. Can you honestly tell me you would be completely in your right mind if you suddenly found out one of them was alive?"

"Don't talk about my parents."

"I'm sorry. But I want you to understand. I have tried so many times to explain this to you but you won't communicate with me. I wasn't trying to abandon you, even though that was the end result. I can't begin to tell you how badly I want your forgiveness. Both of you," she added, glancing in the mirror where Bones stared back at her with a flinty gaze.

Maddock folded his arms, chewed his lip. Finally, he spoke.

"The people who are after us claim to be descended from Black Caesar. In their minds, that means Solomon's ring, and the mines, are theirs."

"Who the bloody hell is Black Caesar?"

Maddock finally looked in her direction, a frown creasing his brow. "What do you mean? I thought you were after Solomon's Mines? Why else would those men have been following you?"

"I am on the trail of the mines." She took a deep breath. She didn't want to tell him anything, or perhaps she didn't want to reveal how little she knew. "H. Rider Haggard spent a great deal of time at the cathedral. I thought he was studying a particular book, but it turns out he was spending time in conversation with a certain priest. He was apparently taken with the man's stories. I know I'm grasping at straws, but Haggard is one of the few avenues I haven't exhausted."

Maddock nodded.

"Are you going to return the favor and tell me about this Black Caesar? It's not like I won't look him up the first chance I get."

"Black Caesar was a slave turned pirate who, we believe, possessed Solomon's ring," Maddock said grudgingly. "He was arrested and sentenced to die. Before his execution, he gave the ring to a man named Israel Hands, who lived out his days in poverty in the area surrounding the cathedral. We thought he might have hidden the ring there or maybe given it to someone."

"Did you find it?"

Maddock shook his head.

"So, what's your next move?"

Maddock gaped at her, disbelief shining in his eyes. "We don't work together anymore, Isla. You work for the Tuatha now. I suppose this is their next big plan? Use the gold from Solomon's mines to what, bribe officials? Buy weapons?"

"No. It's not like that. You don't understand anything."

"I understand enough. You've joined forces with the people who, a few months ago, were trying to kill us."

"I'm wasting my breath with you," she said. Anger welled up inside of her. The fool man wouldn't even hear her out. "I could help you, you know. I'm not a member of the Tuatha, as you seem to think, but I have resources at my disposal. And I've been researching Solomon's Mines. I have a lot to offer, but I'm sure you're too stubborn to accept my help."

"You got that right," Maddock said.

"Fine. Where shall I drop you off?"

"The nearest pub will be fine," Bones said.

Isla pulled to the curb at first sight of a pub. As Maddock unbuckled his seat belt and turned to unlock the door, she made a hasty decision. She reached into her purse and slipped out a tiny metal object. She reached out and grabbed the hem of Maddock's jacket. He froze but didn't turn to look at her. It pained her, but that was exactly what she'd hoped for.

"Please, just consider talking with me some time,"

she said as she clipped the object to his jacket. "I want to make it right."

Maddock gave a shake of his head and exited the car, slamming the door behind him.

"Just be that way, Dane Maddock," she said softly. "Try and shut me out of your life. We'll be seeing each other again very soon."

CHAPTER 25
The Boleyn Tavern, London

The Boleyn was a tavern on Barking Road in London. Reading Maddock's mood, Bones refrained from making puns with the street's name or any jokes about beheading wives. He followed Maddock inside, eager to learn who, exactly, was after them, and what, if anything, Maddock had found behind the secret door.

The tavern was impressive. Lots of old wood and stained glass. The floor was a little sticky and the place could have used some spit and polish, but it was what Bones imagined a London pub would be like—old, with a strong sense of history. They ordered two craft beers and a pizza at the bar, then found an out of the way table. The crowd was sparse this time of day, with only a few men in West Ham Football t-shirts or jerseys occupying a few seats here and there.

They settled in and Maddock filled him in on what had transpired—the descendants of Black Caesar, finding the body of Israel Hands, and the message carved in stone.

"You think H. Rider Haggard took the ring and, I don't know, gave it to his wife?"

"Something like that," Maddock said.

"You think he used it first? Found Solomon's Mines and opened it?"

Maddock shook his head. "Haggard wouldn't have been a young man by then. I don't think he'd have been up to the journey, which is why he planned on giving the ring away."

"Why bother stealing it, then?"

"The legend of King Solomon's mines was his passion, maybe even an obsession. I think he figured out where the mines were, but without the ring he couldn't get inside. And that meant he couldn't prove the legend was true."

Bones rubbed his chin. "So, finding the ring was the

completion of his quest? It satisfied him that he'd been right all along?"

"That's what I think. He knew he couldn't survive the demands of the journey back to Africa. Maybe he couldn't afford to fund an expedition. So, he satisfied himself with the knowledge that he'd assembled all the clues. And he couldn't resist leaving that message with Israel Hands' remains, just to show who had solved the riddle. I guess that had to be enough for him."

"Wouldn't be enough for me," Bones said. "Or you." He and Maddock could back out of this search anytime. Let Isla and the descendants of Caesar fight it out. But the truth was, the two of them were cut from the same cloth as men like Haggard. Treasure hunting was an obsession. Despite the danger, there was no way either of them would give up the chase.

"You're right about that. I've got the bit in my teeth now." Maddock took another drink.

Maddock's phone vibrated. He took it out and spent a minute reading the text message.

"What's up?" Bones asked as Maddock pocketed his phone.

"After Avery and the guys had the encounter at Caesar's rock, Nomi's partner, a woman named Constance, ended up following Avery to work."

"Oops. Bet Tam didn't like that." Tam Broderick was a babe, but she took no crap from anyone.

"Exactly. They detained and questioned her. Didn't learn much except these descendants of Caesar call themselves 'the family' or 'the cousins.' They don't have a name or an oranizational structure as far as she can tell; just a lot of powerful people working with or against each other depending on the circumstances. They all answer to a man they call 'Uncle.' Tam suspects ties to African warlords and terrorists."

"The Trident?" Bones asked.

"No reason to think so. At least, not at the moment."

"I assume these cousins are working together?"

"A few of them are, at least. Anyway, Avery was

burglarized and the artifact stolen. She still has photographs of the code she's trying to decipher, so that's not a problem."

Bones clenched and relaxed his fists. "But that means the *cousins* have it, too."

Maddock nodded. "The race is on." He looked up. "Hold on. I'm going to see if they have a phone I can borrow."

Bones thought that was odd, but he was sure Maddock had his reasons. While his friend headed over to the bar, Bones took out his smartphone and looked up H. Rider Haggard's burial site. The famed author was laid to rest, along with the remains of his wife and other family members, at St. Mary's Church in Ditchingham, a two-and-a-half hour drive from London. Bones found a photograph of the grave marker, which listed the dead who were buried there. It was a close-up photo and he couldn't tell if the remains were buried, or contained in some sort of crypt. He didn't relish the idea of digging up a grave.

Maddock returned, the ghost of a smile playing across his face. He drained his glass and let out a satisfied sigh.

"You going to tell me what that was all about?" Bones asked.

"I just called in an anonymous tip to the Norfolk Constabulary. I wanted them to know someone is going to deface Haggard's grave tonight."

"What the hell did you do that for? I thought Haggard buried the ring with his "beloved soulmate.'"

"I think he did," Maddock said. "But although he loved her, his wife was not his soulmate."

CHAPTER 26
St. Mary's Church, Ditchingham

St. Mary's Church had once been the center of the village of Ditchingham. Built in the fifteenth century, it now dominated a pastoral landscape, sitting alone in the countryside. Its hundred foot tall tower cast a long shadow in the pale moonlight. Ronald thought it might be beautiful in the daylight, but at night, it felt sinister. The weathered grave markers between which he and Cleo passed only added to the haunted aura surrounding the old church.

"Look here. This is a Haggard." Cleo shone his torch on a grave marker that read Lillias Haggard.

Ronald shook his head. "That's his daughter. Follow me."

They made their way to the front door of the church. Cleo kept watch, probably unnecessarily, considering the remote location and relative insignificance of the place, while Ronald picked the lock.

Once inside, a brief search led them to Haggard's crypt. A large rectangle of black marble marked the spot.

"O ye dry bones, hear the word of the Lord. Behold, I will cause breath to enter into you and ye shall live," Ronald read aloud from the script ringing the slab. "The eternal God is thy dwelling place and underneath are the everlasting arms."

"Underneath are the everlasting arms?" Cleo asked. "Makes it sound like…hell."

Ronald nodded but didn't reply. Something else had caught his attention.

"Seven people are buried here?" Cleo asked, echoing his own thoughts. "That's a lot."

"Cremains," Ronald said. "I imagined Haggard burying the ring with his dead wife but perhaps he placed it in her urn?"

"One way to be certain."

Cleo had brought a crowbar with him, and now he

knelt and worked it between the edge of the marble slab and the surrounding tile.

"Break it if you must," Ronald said. "We'll take the ring and leave the urn. When the damage is discovered, they'll find nothing missing."

Just then, the front door banged open and bright lights blinded him.

"Police!" a voice shouted. "Put your hands in the air."

As uniformed men poured into the church, Ronald sighed and raised his hands above his head. The cousins were not going to be happy.

CHAPTER 27
Aldeburgh, England

The cool night breeze ruffled Maddock's hair as he peered out from the copse of buckthorn that stood at the edge of the cemetery. No one was about.

"Okay, Maddock. You've played your mysterious act to the hilt. Tell me what we're doing here," Bones said.

"When Haggard was nineteen, he fell in love with a girl named Mary Elizabeth Jackson. He wanted to marry her, but her father wouldn't allow it until he established himself in a career. He considered them to be secretly engaged, but when he finally proposed, she turned him down and married a wealthy banker instead."

"Ouch."

"Exactly. In his autobiography, he wrote that it was such a crushing blow, he would not have been sorry to depart the world."

"Sounds like you on one of your emo days," Bones said. "Never let a chick get into your head."

Maddock smirked. "Things didn't work out for her. Her husband was a gambling addict who lost everything. The only thing he left her when he died was a case of syphilis."

Bones sucked in a breath between his teeth and winced. "They didn't have penicillin back then, did they?"

"I don't think so. Anyway, she returned to England, where Haggard secretly supported her and her family until her death. Haggard believed his love for her was eternal and that they would be united in the afterlife. A lot of people believe that the immortal queen in his novel, *She*, was based on his true love."

"Holy crap, Maddock. I did not sign up for a course in British Literature. How do you know so much about this?"

"Haggard is the father of the "lost world" adventure genre. I've always loved his books." Maddock didn't have to see Bones to know his friend was rolling his eyes.

"Anyway, Haggard never got over her. He even named one of his daughters Lillias, in her honor. Of course, Lillias wasn't a fan. She referred to the woman as 'Lilith' because of the destructive influence she had on her father."

"Lillias?"

"Her given name was Mary Elizabeth, but she went by..."

"Lilly," Bones finished. "His Lilly of the valley."

"It was spelled with two L's in the message he left," Maddock said.

"Fine. You've convinced me you're a freaking genius." Bones glanced at his watch. "You think it's late enough to get to work?"

Maddock was about to reply in the affirmative when he spotted a glimmer of light on the other side of the cemetery. A figure emerged carrying a flashlight. He recognized her immediately.

"Isla. How in the hell?" Anger boiling inside him, he stalked across the dark graveyard.

"Maddock, a little stealth?" Bones whispered.

Maddock ignored him. As he drew nearer, he saw Isla kneel and begin to dig. A few seconds later, she drew from the earth a small box.

"How did you find us?"

He'd thought to surprise her, but Isla didn't flinch.

"I know about Haggard, too, which means I know about Lilly."

Maddock wasn't buying it. "You couldn't know about the message Haggard left unless you went back to the cathedral, and I doubt you did that considering the chaos we left behind."

"You refuse to accept that I've got some talents of my own," she said, striding over to him and poking him in the chest. "I'm a treasure hunter now, just like you, but you have no respect for me or for what I can do."

"What are you talking about?" Maddock asked. "I just want the ring."

At the mention of the ring, Isla danced backward a few steps. "Let's work together."

"No."

"Come on, Maddock. You can't open Solomon's Mines without the ring. Also, I've got resources at my disposal."

"You really think we can't take the ring if we want it?" Bones appeared behind her.

"Don't come any closer." Isla drew a small pistol and aimed it at the big Cherokee. Maddock noted her steady hand. She was not afraid.

"You won't shoot me," Bones said, taking a step closer. "Your finger's not even on the trigger."

Isla fired a shot, the bullet tearing up the turf a few feet in front of Bones. "It is now. Next time I'll aim just a little bit higher."

"Isla, this is ridiculous. There are others on the trail of the ring and we don't have time to stand here arguing."

"You're correct," Isla said. "So stop being a wankpuffin and help me find the mines."

Maddock couldn't believe he was even considering her offer. Yes, she'd run away when they'd been under attack by the Tuatha de Danaan. He'd assumed she was joining them, but perhaps she was telling the truth, and she'd only been running to safety...to her mother. And he couldn't deny an attraction to her remained. God, she was beautiful, and this newfound confidence only made her more so. But no, he couldn't do it. He had no idea who she was working for. What if this new group were worse than the so-called cousins?

"Give me the ring." He started walking toward her. "I know you won't shoot me."

"Perhaps not," said a new voice from the darkness, "but I will."

A sturdily built man with a shaved head stepped into the faint light cast by the moon and by Isla's flashlight. He held a Colt AR-15 semi-automatic rifle aimed at Bones' chest.

Maddock tensed. The pistol he had taken off of Ronald was tucked into his belt. No way could he draw and fire before this man shot him. Hell, the safety was still on.

"Who the hell are you?" Bones asked. He stood with his hands up, clearly having assessed the situation and seen no strategic advantage to a frontal assault.

"This is Gowan," Isla said. "He's my partner in this."

"So you also work for…" Maddock left the sentence hanging, but Gowan didn't bite.

"None of your concern." He glanced at Isla. "Why are we wasting time with these tossers? You have the ring, don't you?"

Isla raised her eyebrows. "I don't know, actually." She tugged at the lid of the metal box. "Rusted closed. You want to know what's inside? Join our team and we can find out together."

"What are you doing, Isla?" Gowan asked.

"They are experienced treasure hunters. No one in the organization can match them. They can help."

"We couldn't trust them." Gowan's frown flitted from Maddock to Bones and back. He took two steps to move in between Isla and the two men. "They'd betray us first chance they got."

"Not if they gave their word," Isla said over Gowan's shoulder. "If they say they won't betray us, they won't."

"Unlike some people," Bones said.

"Please," Isla said. "We can work together, beat these cousins or whoever they are to the mines, and share the treasure."

Despite himself, Maddock found his resolve crumbling. He wanted to forgive Isla. "Tell us who you're working for and I'll consider it."

"There's nothing to consider." Gowan raised his rifle. Maddock dove to the side as he heard the report of a gunshot.

He hit the soft earth face-first, his ears ringing. The breath left him in a rush, but he felt no pain. Had Gowan missed? He rolled over, grabbing for his pistol, but there was no need.

Gowan lay in a pool of blood, the side of his head ruined. Isla stood over him, pistol hanging limply at her side, her face white as a sheet.

"I can't believe I shot him," she whispered.

"I can't either, but thanks," Bones said, gently taking the pistol from her hand.

"He was going to kill you," she said to Maddock. "I couldn't let him."

Maddock didn't know what to say.

"I've done it now," she said, forcing a weak laugh. "I've made an enemy of the Tuatha and the Sisterhood."

"Sisterhood?" Maddock and Bones said in unison.

"They've joined forces," Isla said. "I'm surprised you've heard of them."

"We've met them before," Maddock said. "I thought they were finished."

"Not by a long shot." Isla stared forlornly at the night sky. "What am I going to do?"

Maddock took a breath, looked at Bones. A small jerk of the head, as if to say, *Do what you've got to do*, was his only reply. Maddock stood, reached out, and took Isla's hand.

"You're coming with us."

CHAPTER 28
Vohipeno, Madagascar

Vohipeno sat nestled on the east bank of the Sandrananta River in southeastern Madagascar just a few miles from the Indian Ocean. The small town and commune had a population of less than 20,000, almost all of whom were farmers, who produced rice and coffee. As they wandered along, Maddock couldn't help but feel he was in another world. Many of the homes were weathered, tin roof shacks set on thick posts to avoid flooding, and virtually all the buildings, even the businesses, were in a similar state. Some looked like they'd been cobbled together from driftwood. The whole town seemed to be graying wood and rust-pitted metal.

"I still think this is a weird place to look for King Solomon's Mines," Bones said. "Is Avery sure she got the code deciphered right?"

"If not, it would be one heck of a coincidence for her to screw up the code and still get a coherent message out of it," Maddock said.

"It's roughly the proper distance from Israel to fit the legends, and Madagascar is rich in resources," Isla said.

Since the incident at Lilly Archer's grave, Isla had buried herself in research. After relieving Gowan of his wallet and smartphone in order to hopefully make him more difficult for police to identify, they'd fled the country. Fortunately, Avery had decoded the message before their departure, giving them a place to head to.

Maddock had some idea of what Isla was going through. Taking a life, even justifiably, took a toll on a person. She would need time to deal with it. Her struggle with what she'd done had gone a long way toward smoothing over relations between her, Maddock, and Bones, especially since she'd admitted to placing a tracker on Maddock's jacket when she'd picked them up outside the cathedral.

"Also, our research seems to support a possible

connection. Rather, Jimmy's research supports it," she added.

Maddock nodded. They'd called upon his old friend, Jimmy Letson, to see if he could find any connection between King Solomon's Mines and the island of Madagascar. He had uncovered a remarkable, yet little-known legend called the "Malagasy Secret." Some Malagasies believed that they were of Israelite descent, and that their forebears were seafaring members of Israel's "lost tribe." Furthermore, local lore amongst these tiny pockets of Judaism held that Madagascar was, in fact, the biblical land of Ophir, the home of King Solomon's Mines, and that Madagascar provided many of the building materials for King Solomon's temple, including gold and rosewood. Curiously, he'd also turned up reports that Madagascar had been considered by France in the late 1700s and the Nazis as a dumping ground for "undesirable" citizens.

"And then there's the fact that the translation included one of the bits of scripture found on H. Rider Haggard's tomb," Isla said. "The secret lies here. I'm certain of it."

"Let's just hope the people here are willing to talk." Maddock pointed to a rickety, whitewashed wooden building. The Star of David was painted in blue above the doorway. They entered the makeshift synagogue, where they were greeted by Rakoto, a robust man dressed in traditional Malagasy clothing. He greeted them warmly, shaking each person's hand in a powerful grip. Maddock was relieved that the man spoke fluent English. He was prepared to converse in French, a language spoken among the educated citizenry of Madagascar, but if the man had only spoken Malagasy, they'd have been stuck trying to make use of an online translation program.

"You're not what I expected," Bones said after introductions had been made.

"Oh?" Rakoto's gray eyebrows twitched with amusement. "You thought to meet a skinny white man with silly sideburns?"

"Something like that," Bones said, chuckling.

"For some reason, my hair will not grow that way." Rakoto laughed, tugging at a patch of close-cropped, curly hair at his graying temple. "Now, what can I do for you?"

"We're archaeologists," Maddock said. "We are on the trail of something...unusual."

Rakoto looked like a child trying his first taste of Scotch Whisky. "King Solomon's Mines."

"We realize it sounds far-fetched," Isla interjected, "but some dangerous people are taking this legend seriously. If there is any truth at all to this legend, we need to protect it from them."

"Two Americans, one...Irishwoman?" Rakoto asked.

"Scottish, actually," Isla said.

Rakoto nodded. "For whom do you work?"

"Bones and I are connected with a special CIA task force," Maddock said. That was technically true, although their connection to the Myrmidons was no longer official. "We've engaged Ms. Mulheron's services for her expertise."

"I would prefer not to get involved."

Maddock reached into his pocket and took out a heavy iron ring and held it up for Rakoto to see the signet. There, in brass, were two interlocked triangles forming a six-pointed star. A tiny sapphire lay in the space between each point.

Rakoto gasped. "That is never the ring..." He trailed off, unable to finish his sentence.

Maddock understood. There was something about the ring. It had a presence, for lack of a better term. You could *feel* it as if it had a life of its own. The moment he'd touched it, he'd known it was the ring of Solomon.

"It's real. Please help us if you can."

Rakoto let out a long, tired sigh. "I know very little, save the legends."

"We're interested in anything you can tell us," Maddock said. "Even if it is not definitive."

"Very well. Please have a seat." They sat down on blankets on the floor and Rakoto began his story.

"Some Malagasy Jews believe we came to the island on Noah's Ark. As if the ark landed in Africa." He let out a rich laugh, while Maddock and Bones exchanged a knowing glance, one that Isla did not miss. She quirked an eyebrow and Maddock shook his head and gestured toward Rakoto, who continued talking. "Among most of our number, the tradition holds that our common ancestor was a man called Alitawarat, or 'Ali Torah.' He was originally from Jerusalem and his first language was Hebrew. He served King Solomon, and discovered the bounty of Madagascar. While the specifics might not be precisely accurate, there is reason to believe that we have an ancient Hebrew heritage. The practice of circumcision, for example, has been a tradition long before missionaries visited our island. Many isolated communities called themselves the 'Descendants of Abraham.' He went on to list other examples of the Madagascar-Hebrew connection. "And then, of course, there is the sacred rock of Alakamisy-Ambohimaha."

"What's that?" Bones asked.

"It is a boulder upon which Hebrew letters have been engraved. You will pass it on your way to Vatumasina."

Isla tilted her head. "Vatumasina."

"It is a royal village where the protectors of the Malagasy secret reside. If anyone can tell you more than mere legend, it will be them."

"Would they speak with us?" Maddock asked.

"They will meet with anyone. But you must ask in the proper form, else they will dismiss you out of hand."

"What's the proper form?" Bones asked.

Rakoto shrugged. "No one in living memory has asked properly. If you manage it, you will be the first."

CHAPTER 29
Vohipeno, Madagascar

Nomi grimaced at the abject poverty all around her. How could people live in such squalor? Nearby, a group of children were busy spreading out rice to dry in the sun. One little girl looked up at her and flashed a shy smile. Nomi ignored her. She hated children.

Ronald and Cleo flanked her. The cousins were not well pleased with any of them in light of recent events. Nomi was being blamed for Constance's disappearance. Some in the family had insinuated that Nomi had killed her; a few had even accused her outright. Cleo and Ronald were in disgrace. The family had seen to it that they'd been allowed to leave England, and the charges of breaking and entering dropped. Still, they had failed. All three had been instructed to proceed directly to Uncle's compound. None had followed the order, knowing what it likely meant for them.

"You are certain of the decoding?" Ronald asked, looking around at the unlikely surroundings.

"My professor friend is certain. And he is also certain that this village has a strong connection to the legends of King Solomon's Mines in Madagascar."

"I didn't know there were any connections," Cleo said.

"That is a good thing. It means few, if any, have searched here."

"Which would explain why the mines have not been found." Cleo nodded thoughtfully.

"It also means the family is unlikely to look for us here," Ronald added.

They passed a row of colorfully-dressed people selling produce in the shade of a dilapidated building. A little boy hurried over to them, bearing a basket of apples. They all shook their heads. When he turned away, eyes downcast, Cleo stole an apple out of his basket. He took a bite and grinned. "What?" he asked, seeing Nomi's frown. "What are they going to do about it?"

"I'm more concerned about you drawing unnecessary attention. If the family learns we are here, people might remember the foreign bully who steals apples from little children."

Cleo considered this for a moment, then nodded.

"There's a great deal you haven't told us," Ronald said to Nomi.

"Such as?" she asked, only half-listening.

"Such as how you plan on getting inside the mines without the ring."

"Dane Maddock has the ring."

Ronald's eyes went wide. "How do you know this?"

"A body was found at the grave of one Mary Elizabeth Archer, and the earth was disturbed as if something had been dug up."

"And we care because?" Cleo asked.

"If you had done even a modicum of research, you would have learned that Archer was Haggard's one true love, and that she went by the name Lilly." The two men gaped at her. "The incident at the graveyard happened the same night you were arrested. It is obvious what happened. Maddock learned about Lilly; you did not."

"So, we catch up to Maddock, and take the ring from him." Ronald cracked his knuckles. "I relish the opportunity to pay him back."

Nomi nodded. "And if we find the mines first, we simply wait and take the ring from him."

"If we recover the ring and find the mines, Uncle will have to forgive us. We will be the first among the cousins." Cleo stared off into the distance, a faint smile playing across his lips.

Nomi kept her silence. She wasn't confident that Uncle would react in that way. She could not recall a single time he had forgiven someone who had failed as badly as they. Of course, none had ever been given the opportunity. They usually ended up being forced to participate in his "games" and those never ended well for anyone but Uncle. If they reached the mines, and found what she expected to find, she would not need Uncle or any of the family. She would be a queen.

CHAPTER 30
Vatumasina, Madagascar

Maddock saw nothing royal about the village Vatumasina. Located only a short distance from Vohipeno, it looked no different. The same dilapidated shacks and commonly dressed citizens. The people were friendly, to be certain, but nothing felt royal.

"This is as disappointing as the sacred rock," Bones said.

Maddock nodded. They'd stopped at Alakamisy-Ambohimaha. As Rakoto has said, it was a boulder inscribed with Hebrew letters. Three of them to be exact, and no matter how Maddock arranged them and what vowels he tried to insert, he couldn't come up with a word that seemed to have any significance. Isla planned on continuing to work on it, but he didn't hold out much hope for success.

After asking around, Maddock found someone who understood his limited French well enough to guide them to the people he sought: a group of elders the villager called "Les rois et scribes" or "the kings and scribes."

The kings and scribes met them outside a squat stone building. The structure was old, but had been fitted with a steel door that was secured with a heavy padlock. The men stood in a line, arms folded, staring daggers at the newcomers. All twelve wore the traditional lamba, a rectangular cloth wrapped around the body, over white robes, and each wore a pillbox hat of red or yellow. Maddock wondered if there was some significance to the color of the hat—perhaps one color denoted a king and another a scribe? Before he could ponder the question further, a wrinkled, bespectacled man spoke.

"What business have you with the kings and scribes?"

Maddock had been considering how to approach this ever since their meeting with Rakoto. He had no idea what the "proper form" of addressing the men might be, and internet searches had proved as fruitless as one might expect, considering no one had ever stumbled upon the proper words. He decided to start with scripture.

"We seek Ophir, from which 420 talents of gold were brought to King Solomon," he said, paraphrasing 1 Kings 9.28.

The man's expression didn't change.

"Speak the words."

Crap. It had been too much to hope that he'd guess it on the first try. Of course others had probably tried this same scripture. Perhaps they could be persuaded.

"We seek to protect the mines from dangerous people who would put the wealth to ill use."

The man held up a finger. "Speak the words," he said, and held up two fingers. The implication was clear. Three strikes and you're out.

In desperation, Maddock took out the ring and held it up for all to see. An audible gasp rippled through the assembly. A few flinched, while others took an involuntary step forward.

"We have Solomon's ring. Help us."

The man swallowed hard, put up a third finger, and said, in a choked voice, "Speak the words." Maddock thought he heard a note of pleading his time, as if the fellow wanted him to succeed.

Bones took a step forward. For a moment, Maddock worried that his friend was about to do something violent, but instead, Bones spoke in a loud, clear voice.

"O ye dry bones, hear the word of the Lord. Behold, I will cause breath to enter into you and ye shall live."

It was the scripture found on Haggard's grave. The same words that Avery and Corey had translated from the artifact recovered on Caesar's rock. Could this be the key?

The faces of the kings and scribes relaxed, and their leader gave a curt nod.

"It suffices." He managed a nervous smile. "I am

called Princio. You must surrender your weapons."

Upon their arrival in Madagascar, they'd managed to acquire pistols through a shady dealer. They handed them over, along with their belt knives, and waited as they were frisked. Isla offered up her pistol but Princio shook his head.

"The woman must wait outside," he said.

"She comes with us," Maddock protested.

"It's fine," Isla said. "We have bigger battles to fight than one against the patriarchy. My feminism can handle the slight if it's for a greater cause."

Maddock gave a reluctant nod and waited as one of the men unlocked the door and held it open for them.

"Follow the labyrinth," Princio said.

Maddock took the lead and followed the narrow corridor as it spiraled inward toward the center of the building. Along the way he noticed carvings in the floor—words in Hebrew, the menorah, and finally, at the very end of the labyrinth, a tiny room. A skylight permitted a narrow beam of sunlight to shine down on a familiar symbol etched into the floor—Solomon's Seal. He and Bones waited expectantly as Princio and another man grasped invisible handholds in the seal and lifted it. It came free like a manhole cover.

"Inside," Princio instructed.

Maddock saw handholds carved into the rough rock. He'd made much more challenging climbs, and if the old men could do it, so could he. He descended quickly, hopping out of the way of Bones, who hit the ground a few seconds after him.

"Wonder why they took us all the way down here." Bones said.

"I guess we will find out." Maddock glanced up, expecting to see the kings and scribes following them down. Instead, he watched as, like a solar eclipse, the light from above vanished as the seal was dragged back into place, sealing them off from the outside world.

Rakoto couldn't help but feel shaken by the

conversation he'd had with the three foreigners. It wasn't that they were interested in Solomon's Mines. That was hardly out of the ordinary in this part of the world, though it wasn't so common in Madagascar. It was the ring that had him rattled.

He could tell at a glance that it was ancient, and it fit the description of Solomon's ring. But what was more, he could *feel* it. He had never before been in the presence of such a holy object. The spirit of God, he supposed. But it hadn't made him feel the way he felt in worship. Its presence was…unsettling. He had felt only relief when they finally left.

Hours later, he sat there in the dim light, staring at the wall. The late afternoon sun cast a beam of golden light through the open doorway. It was getting time to go home. Rakoto stood but before he could take a step, a shadow announced the approach of a visitor.

A woman stepped inside. She was attractive, with high cheekbones and big eyes, but the sinister expression on her face deprived her of much of her beauty. Two men entered in her wake, closing the door and taking up positions in front of it. Rakoto did not miss the bulges of poorly concealed weapons.

"Welcome." Rakoto was certain they could hear the fear in his voice. "How may I help you?"

"We need information." She ran a hand through her close-cropped hair.

Rakoto waited, heart in his throat.

"Have you had any visitors today?"

"I have," he said in a hoarse grunt. He cleared his throat, forced a measure of confidence into his tone. "Two sets of visitors in one day. More than I usually receive in a month."

"Dane Maddock." It was not a question.

Rakoto saw no point in lying to these people. In fact, he suspected it would be in his best interest to cooperate fully. He had no stake in this foolish legend quest.

"American with blond hair and blue eyes? Traveling with a big Native American and a Scottish girl?"

The woman frowned slightly, then nodded. "Tell me everything."

Rakoto recounted his conversation of earlier in the day. The woman listened, nodding impatiently. She interrupted him only once.

"He had a ring?" she asked, her voice sharp like the crack of a whip. "Describe it."

He described the ring, omitting the way he felt when he looked at it. He had a feeling these people had no time for such nonsense.

The woman turned and looked at her companions, who flashed twin smiles, predatory like lions on the hunt.

Rakoto's heart raced. Clearly this ring was important to them. But was it important enough to silence him? He couldn't believe the turn of events in his life that had led him to even contemplate such a thing. He was a simple man. He wanted no part of dangerous people.

"Do you know where they went?"

"Yes. At least, I know where I told them to go." He told her about the royal village of Vatumasina and of the legends that connected it with Hebrew tradition. She probably didn't need to know all of that, but he felt the need to keep talking, to forestall the moment when they decided what to do about him.

When he finished, the woman stared at him for ten heart-stopping seconds.

"Anything else? Anything at all you forgot to tell me?"

Rakoto considered. There was nothing else, but he wanted to keep talking, make himself useful, to prolong with might be the last moments of his life. But to tell her more might suggest he had held something back. He looked around for a weapon, knowing there was none. And even if there was, what could a man of peace do against three armed assailants who looked as if they knew what they were about? He shook his head.

"I have told you everything," he rasped, his throat a desert. He breathed a sigh of relief as the woman turned toward the door. "Blessings be upon you."

One of the men reached for his pistol. Rakoto took a step back.

"No," the woman said. "The killing could be used to track us." She turned to Rakoto. "If anyone else comes, you have had no unusual visitors. That includes Maddock."

"I understand," Rakoto breathed.

He stood there, frozen in place, until long after the three had gone. Finally, he summoned the strength to walk to the door and steal a glance outside. No sign of them. He closed the door, locked it behind him, and hurried home. He hoped he never heard another word about Solomon's Mines for the rest of his life.

"**What the hell** is going on?" Bones stared up into the darkness at the spot where they'd just been shut inside the chamber. "How about I climb back up there?"

"Hold off on that for now," Maddock said. "I'm not sure they're trying to trap us here. Besides, they've got our weapons."

"What makes you think they're not up to something?"

"I don't know. A feeling, I guess." He reached into his pocket for his Maglite, then froze. "Don't turn on your light," he said to Bones.

Bones didn't argue. His friend could usually recognize the tone in Maddock's voice that said, *trust me.*

The floor had begun to sparkle. A faint cloud of silvery blue specks led back into the darkness.

"Maybe they wanted us to follow the path."

"I wish we'd gotten a look at the space around us first. No telling what we're walking into."

"I think we need to stick to the path. Why else would they black out the light above us?" He had a feeling that, if they turned on their lights, the path might vanish and not return anytime soon.

"In that case, you lead the way, bro."

They followed the sparkling path, careful to keep to the center in case Maddock was correct that sticking to the path was essential. In the darkness, it almost felt as if they were standing still. Finally they rounded a corner and a brighter glow illuminated their surroundings.

The sparkling path on which they walked led into a small cave. A figure sat facing them. Maddock tensed, but relaxed when he saw it was a statue of a robed man seated cross-legged, as if meditating. On the ground in front of him, Solomon's Seal shone inside a blue circle of light.

"Uh, Maddock?" Bones said. "Is that a flashlight in your pocket or do you think that statue is really hot?"

"What?" Maddock looked down to see that the Maglite in his pocket had somehow turned on. But it wasn't his flashlight.

"The ring," he said. "It's glowing."

He took Solomon's Ring and held it out in his upturned palms. The seal shone with dancing blue light, the twin of the symbol carved into the floor.

"This is odd," Maddock said.

"Do you think this is the entrance to the mine?" Bones asked, a touch of doubt in his voice.

"Doubtful. This isn't mining country."

"The ring is supposed to be the key to the mine. Why don't you try and open the door just in case?"

Maddock wasn't sure what to do. He slipped the ring onto his finger. A chill passed over him, raising goosebumps on his flesh. A sense of a strange presence filled the air around him, as if someone else were there.

Feeling foolish, he made a fist, held out his hand, and said, "Open."

Nothing happened.

"Try, 'open sesame,'" Bones offered.

"I don't think that's the trick." Maddock let his hand fall to the side, but he didn't remove the ring. He still couldn't escape that feeling that they weren't alone.

"You know what this reminds me of?" Bones said. "A séance." He pointed to the symbol on the floor. "You've got what looks like a pentagram. You've got the dude sitting there waiting to talk to the spirit world…"

Maddock nodded. "I think you might be onto something."

"Well, I am a freaking genius, as you well know."

Maddock laughed. "Let's join our friend on the floor. Don't touch the circle."

"Dude, you hook up with one ghost hunter and suddenly you're an expert?"

"Just a hunch. But hey, if you want to cross the circle, be my guest."

Bones looked doubtfully at the seal on the floor. "Nah, I'm good."

They took up spots on the floor outside the circle. Maddock rested his hand on his lap and looked at the statue. "I guess we can at least adopt a spirit of welcoming, like we did at the séance in Williamsburg."

A silence settled over them as they waited, anticipating. Nothing changed. He racked his brain, trying to remember what Kendra and her ghost hunter friends had done to connect with the spirit world. One of the men had rung a bell three times. He had no bell to ring. The only thing he had on him at the moment that was made of metal was his Maglite.

And the ring!

He took out his flashlight and tapped it against the ring three times. On the third tap, light flared from the ring. A bright blue beam shot out from the ring and struck the statue in the chest.

A shroud of flickering blue light surrounded the statue. It swirled and pulsed, gradually forming into the ghost of a man. Maddock and Bones stared at the strange apparition as it looked from one of them to the other.

And then it spoke a single word.

"Ask."

Maddock could only think of one question.

"How do we find King Solomon's Mines?"

Maddock gazed at the spirit thing, amazed that this was even happening. What was this thing? An actual ghost? Something the ring had conjured?

The lips moved.

"From the center of the Sacred Twelve, within the Houses of the Seven, across the river, through the bad water, between the breasts of Sheba, you shall return as the wise king did. Speak the words and ye shall enter."

"What words?" Bones asked.

But the spirit was already flickering like a television set losing its signal.

And then it was gone.

"Dropped connection," Bones said. "Need a new cell

phone tower out here."

Maddock nodded grimly. "Those were directions to Solomon's Mines, for certain," he said. "Haggard mentions the Breasts of Sheba and bad water."

"Is what he gave us enough, though? You've got to figure people have been looking for Sheba's boobs for a while now."

"The starting point has got to be key. Figure out what the Sacred Twelve is and go from there."

"If you say so. I guess now we get to find out if those dudes are planning on letting us out or if we need to use the back door."

Bones stood, knuckled his back, and headed back the way they had come. "I've got to admit, I expected fancier digs for Solomon's ghostly gatekeeper or whatever he is." Bones looked around as he walked. "I guess we've gotten spoiled."

"Bones! Stay on the path!" Maddock shouted.

Too late. Bones had strayed a bit too far to his left. His booted foot came down outside the specks of blue light. With a loud crack of shattering stone and a shout of surprise, he fell.

Maddock reached out and caught Bones by the back of his jacket as the big man struggled to regain his balance. He hauled Bones back into the center of the pathway.

"What the hell?"

"The floor gave way," Maddock said. "I think it must be a false floor on either side of the path. No telling what you'd be falling into or onto."

"Nice of them to warn us." Bones flashed an angry look at the ceiling.

"Probably a way of weeding out the unworthy or something like that," Maddock said. "Let's get out of here. And don't step off the path again."

"Don't worry. For the first time in my life I'm going to walk the straight and narrow."

They climbed back up and Bones roughly shoved the cover aside. The kings and scribes stood there waiting for them. If they were offended by his rough treatment of the seal, they did not say so.

"Thanks for telling us about the floor," Bones said. "Good thing I didn't tear my jeans."

"You found what you were looking for, I assume?" Princio said.

"We learned something," Maddock said. "I don't suppose you have anything to add?"

"None of us knows the secrets. It is believed that only one of a few sacred relics can turn the key, if you will."

"Thank you for showing us," Maddock said, disappointed that they hadn't learned more. Surely, whoever or whatever had laid this path before them had known what they were doing and provided adequate information. They'd have to hope for the best.

"Any of you know what the Sacred Twelve are?" Bones asked. "And how do we get to the middle of them?"

The men all sprang back as if Bones were a viper about to strike.

"You must not speak of what you hear in the sanctum." Princio raised his hands as if to ward off their words.

"Really? Who made that rule?"

"It is older than memory."

"Maybe you remembered it wrong. We've got the ring, so the way I see it, that puts us in charge." The men were inching away, but Bones continued on. "We need to find the Sacred Twelve, the bad water, and if any of you have ever poked your face into Sheba's cleavage, it would be cool if you could draw us a map." He said the last to their backs as they hurried away.

"Nice, Bones," Maddock said.

"They were pissing me off," Bones said. "We show up with Solomon's Ring and they won't tell us jack."

"I guess we're on our own again. Let's see if they'll give us our weapons back."

That proved to be no problem. The kings and scribes

were more than eager for the two men to be on their way. They had lost all semblance of royal demeanor, anxiously shoving the weapons into their hands and ushering them out the door, where Isla waited.

"Well?" Her green eyes blazed. Clearly she hadn't been as all right with being left behind as she had pretended.

"We spoke to a ghost," Maddock said.

"Don't wind me up, Maddock. I'm not in the mood."

"I'm not kidding." He quickly recounted what had transpired inside, omitting the bit where Bones almost fell to his death.

"The Sacred Twelve," she said, taking out her phone and performing a quick search. "Sacred Twelve..." she mumbled. "Here's something. The Twelve Sacred Hills of Imerima."

"Never heard of them," Bones said.

"These hills are sacred to the Marina people of Madagascar. Located in the central highlands, the sacred hills are sites of many ancient capitals and the tombs of important historical figures. Many leaders of renown were also born in these hills. According to legend, King Andrianjaka declared these hills sacred. He had twelve wives, and kept one at each sacred hill."

"That's the way to do it," Bones said.

Isla rolled her eyes and kept reading. "There are, in fact, more than twelve hills that currently claim sacred status, but there are twelve that are generally agreed upon."

"So, we draw a bunch of lines and find what's in the middle?" Bones suggested.

"It's worth a try," Maddock said. "But how about we go somewhere less conspicuous before we continue the discussion?"

They found an out of the way spot, sat down, and began consulting maps of the Twelve Sacred Hills.

"I don't get it," Bones said. "These sacred hills aren't a secret. Why wouldn't someone have found the clue by now?"

"If the ring was needed in order to receive the spirit's message, then it's possible no one knows the significance of the hills," Maddock said.

He scanned a map he had called up on his phone. "This would be easier with a paper map, but maybe if we were to draw lines between the various hills and see if there's a spot they all meet?"

He saved a screen capture of the map, opened it in a new app, and began drawing lines.

"Anything?" Bones asked.

"No joy. The lines don't all meet in the same spot."

Bones glanced down at the map Maddock had been drawing on. "You know, if a few of those hills were in slightly different spots, you could make Solomon's Seal."

Maddock's heart began to race. "Bones, I'd say you're a genius, but you only make these brilliant deductions when you aren't trying."

"How's that brilliant? The hills are in the wrong places."

"Isla said there's some dispute as to which of the hills are the true, original Sacred Twelve."

"I see what you're getting at. Isla, are there any alternatives that fit the bill?"

"Already on it," Isla said. "Let's start by marking the hills that are considered certainties, then we'll play with the others."

They set to work, trying out alternatives, marking the spots on the map, and lining them up. Finally, just as Bones predicted, they had marked out twelve hills that formed the points of Solomon's Seal: the six points of the star and the six jewels.

"We did it!" Isla said. She gave Maddock's hand a squeeze. He didn't respond. There was still a distance there that hadn't yet been bridged.

"Hey, how about a little credit, here?" Bones asked.

"Fine. You're very smart," she said. "The question is, how are we going to identify the exact center? That could be important."

"Try taking the longitude and latitude of the

northernmost and southernmost points," Maddock said.

"And split the difference between the two points of latitude," Isla said, catching on immediately. "Let me see." She performed the necessary calculations, then entered the new coordinates. "Here goes nothing."

The result came up immediately.

Maddock grinned. "Bingo."

CHAPTER 32
The Rova of Antananarivo, Madagascar

The Rova of Antananarivo was a royal palace complex that served as the home of the rulers of the Kingdom of Imerina in the 17th and 18th centuries, as well as of the rulers of the Kingdom of Madagascar in the 19th century. Located in the central highland city of Antananarivo, it stood atop the highest point on Analamanga, formerly the highest of Antananarivo's many hills, in the exact spot their calculations had identified. Over time, many of the structures were rebuilt or expanded, and the complex grew until 1995 when it burned. Since then, many of the tombs and main buildings had been restored.

"You are now standing at an altitude of 4,760 feet," the tour guide said. "This hill is considered the birthplace of Antananarivo. The name means 'The City of a Thousand,' so-called for the thousand soldiers stationed here by King Andrianjaka in 1610."

As the guide went on, pointing out the 360-degree view of the city below, the patches of green that marked rice fields, and notable structures like the palace of the prime minister, Maddock scanned the top of the hill, looking for anything promising. He assumed that any place or clue related to the mine would predate the construction of the Rova. They'd searched for accounts of caves, passageways, even underground bodies of water beneath the Rova, but had found nothing. It seemed this was their best option.

The guide led them into the palace of the queen. Here, only the walls had survived the fire, but a new roof had been added on. As the guide discussed the history and architecture, Maddock and Bones looked around for clues, but nothing leaped out at them.

"Not looking good," Bones said softly. "If we need freaking ground-penetrating radar..."

Just then, Maddock's attention returned to what the

guide was saying.

"The king also selected the site and design of the royal tombs, which he named Trano Masina Fitomiandalana. The name translates to 'Seven Sacred Houses Arranged in Order.' Also…"

Maddock heard nothing after that. He, Bones, and Isla turned to one another and said, "Houses of the Seven!"

The guide led them down to the tombs, which had been restored after the fire, and Maddock's hope waned. If there had been a clue there, what if it had been lost, or discovered already?

"What part of this space is original?" he asked the guide.

"The walls, the floor, some of the tombs, and the remains of course." He smiled and winked at Isla, who returned his grin but without much enthusiasm.

"Focus on that," Maddock whispered. They spread out, inspecting the tombs that had been set in a straight line. Maddock kept an eye out for any symbols that might be related to King Solomon, but nothing leaped out at him.

A scripture was engraved in stone at the foot of every tomb. Centuries of foot traffic had worn them down until they were scarcely visible. Maddock took the time to inspect each one. Though they were at least partially illegible, he could make out words in French here and there; enough that he was able to identify the passage from the Bible. When he reached the last tomb, he gave a start.

"…breath and you shall live," he translated. The same scripture from Haggard's grave, the passage that had been the key to admission to the sanctum in the royal village.

The tour group was now filing out of the tombs. Isla cast a quizzical look in his direction. With a jerk of his head, he indicated that she and Bones should keep moving. He'd hang back and see if this clue bore fruit.

When everyone had gone, he knelt to inspect the

inscription. It was carved into a stone disc. Checking to make sure no one was about, he took out his knife and worked around the edges of the disc until it came free. He lifted it out and brushed aside the silt and sand to reveal images carved into the bedrock.

A stylized sun sank over the rough-hewn shapes of a lion, a bird, and an elephant. The elephant's trunk wrapped around its body. The bird's head was thrown back, its beak open wide, as if devouring the sun. Below them, etched so faintly he almost didn't notice it, was the Seal of Solomon.

"What does this mean?" he whispered. He took a moment to snap a few photos of the images, and then covered it back over with sand before replacing the stone.

As he hurried out of the tombs to catch up with his friends, a torrent of thoughts surged through his mind. What significance could the animals have? Who had carved the symbol there? Had it been done during the construction of the palace, or was it much older? Could the tombs have been built for the purpose of concealing it from the unworthy, with the scripture carved there as a guidepost for those in the know?

"Don't overthink it, Maddock," he said to himself. "Just follow the clues."

CHAPTER 33
Tsingy de Bemaraha, Madagascar

The Tsingy de Bemaraha National park was located in northwestern Madagascar just north of the famed Avenue of the Baobabs. Its unique geological makeup had led to the formation of tsingys—karstic plateaus in which erosion had formed forests of limestone needles.

Maddock could not believe his eyes as they wound among them. He'd never seen anything quite like them. He gazed up at the tall, spiked columns of limestone that rose high above the sparse tree line.

"This gives new meaning to 'petrified forest,'" Bones observed.

"It's magnificent," Isla agreed.

"If King Solomon's Mines are hidden somewhere in here, it's no wonder they've never been discovered. This place is a warren of caverns and crevasses. A man could get lost in here and never find his way out," Maddock said.

Isla smirked. "Only because he'd be too stubborn to ask directions."

"What does tsingy mean, anyway?" Bones asked.

"It's a Malagasy word that translates to 'where one cannot walk barefoot.'" Isla's eyes flitted toward the ground as she spoke. "And I can see why."

"Looks like we're almost there," Bones said, checking his GPS. "I hope this is the place, or else we've come a long-ass way for nothing." He cast a meaningful glance at Isla, who glared back.

"It's the right place. I'm certain of it."

The clue hidden at the Rova of Antananarivo, the images of the lion, bird, and elephant, had confounded them at first. And then Isla had found a tourist's photograph of three unusual-looking rock formations in the middle of Tsingy de Bemaraha. There was no denying the shapes bore a strong resemblance to those in the carving. What was more, they were oriented in such a way that the setting sun would sink behind them.

What had sealed it for Maddock, though, was what lay in between the Rova and the rock formations. Drawing a straight line from one to the other, the line started at the Rova, the center of the Sacred Twelve, the House of the Seven. It passed over the Ikopa River, and then through the Analavory Geysers, carbon dioxide driven, cold water geysers that could definitely qualify as "bad water."

It had been at this point where Maddock's pitch had been derailed by Bones, who couldn't stop laughing and talking about "Anal Lovery Guy-zers." Things had only gotten worse when Isla corrected his spelling, prompting a barrage of "Anal Avery" jokes and a vow to give Maddock's sister a new nickname when they returned home.

After much too long a delay, Maddock had resumed his analysis. "Haggard places the Breasts of Sheba forty leagues from the river. That's approximately two hundred-twenty kilometers. Which would place them about here." He clicked on the satellite map and zoomed in on two very round hills, each almost the twin of the other. "I think these could qualify as the Breasts of Sheba." The others had found his argument persuasive, which brought them to this spot, on the southern edge of the national park.

The sun was high overhead by the time they located the rock formations. Maddock mopped sweat from his brow, took a swig of water, and passed it along to Isla, who sipped sparingly. She offered it to Bones, but he declined.

"Pop a stone in your mouth," he said, opening his mouth so they could see a round pebble. "Keeps you from getting thirsty."

"But it doesn't keep you from dehydrating," Maddock said. "Take a drink. I won't have you slowing us down on the climb."

"Last one up buys dinner," Bones said. He took a swallow from the canteen and handed it back to

Maddock. "You don't have to play if you don't want to," he said to Isla.

"I've done my share of climbing," she said. "And I don't have to drag three hundred pounds of fat arse all the way up there."

"Three hundred? Chick, don't get a job at the fair guessing people's weight."

Isla laughed. "Which one do we climb first? The lion symbolizes God as well as kings."

"But if that's a Jesus fish, we'll have wasted a lot of effort." Bones pointed up at the odd formation.

"I think it's the fish, but not for the reason you mention," Maddock said. "Remember the last part of the clue?"

"Speak the words and enter?" Isla said.

"No, the other part."

Bones ran a hand through his long hair, frowning. "You shall return as the wise king did."

Maddock nodded. "The wise king is obviously Solomon. I was reading through some of Isla's research. There's a story about how he once lost his ring and was forced to wander the world as a commoner until he got it back again."

Isla clapped herself on the forehead. "He found the ring inside the mouth of a fish."

"What do you say?" Maddock asked.

"It's worth a try," Bones said. "Let's go."

It was a strenuous climb, but not particularly challenging for any of the three. In the end, Bones reached the top a few seconds ahead of Maddock, who slowed himself down by constantly checking on Isla. As it turned out, the young woman didn't need help, and almost finished ahead of Maddock. Both men were impressed by her skill and Bones even offered to let her off the hook for dinner, an offer she flatly declined.

"A bet is a bet. But I choose the restaurant."

"Holy crap," Bones muttered, "now we're in for it. Don't Scots eat sheep scrotums and cat crap?"

"No, that's the Irish. Now, where do we go from

here?"

Maddock pointed down the steep slope that led into the shadowy mouth of the fish.

"That way."

"It is them!" Ronald raised his pistol and took aim at the three figures standing atop the rock formation high above them.

Nomi smacked his hand down. "Don't waste your shot. You'd never hit any of them at this distance without a rifle. All you would accomplish would be to alert them to our presence. We've worked too hard for that to happen."

Ronald gave her a hard look but did not argue.

They'd followed Maddock's trail, first to the synagogue and then to the so-called royal village. The fools who called themselves "kings and scribes" had not denied that Maddock and Bonebrake had been there, along with their new female companion, but the men swore that they had told the outsiders nothing.

Cleo had killed two of them before they finally broke down and told all that they knew.

Maddock and Bonebrake had descended into an underground sanctuary where they supposedly communed with spirits. Nomi had considered inspecting the place, but the kings and scribes had been a bit too eager to oblige. Probably there were booby traps down there. Instead, she'd focused on extracting information.

Upon emerging from the chamber, Bonebrake had asked about the "Sacred Twelve," "bad water," and the Breasts of Sheba. Afterward, one of the scribes had shadowed them and overheard them talking about paying a visit to the Rova of Antananarivo. Hot on their heels, Nomi had nearly caught up with them. Plenty of people at the Rova remembered the big Native American showing a great deal of interest in the tombs.

Ronald had finally made himself useful by identifying a fragment, in French, of the same scripture found on H. Rider Haggard's grave, and finding the clue hidden beneath it. Learning about this rock formation had been a stroke of good luck, and even then they were not certain they were in the right place. It was what an American football fan would call a "Hail Mary." But Maddock's presence here seemed to confirm that they'd made the correct call.

"What do you want to do?" Cleo asked.

"We wait a few minutes and then we go up after them. If the mine is up there, Maddock will have opened it. I am certain of it."

CHAPTER 34

The light grew dim as they descended into the mouth of the fish. A series of weathered bumps that might have been steps a few thousand years ago provided footholds as they worked their way down into shadow until at last they stood on level ground. Maddock looked around. He hadn't expected a flashing sign pointing them to King Solomon's Mines, but he thought they'd encounter more than a blank wall.

"This has to be it, doesn't it?" Isla asked.

"I suppose," he said doubtfully. "Those steps had to lead somewhere." He slipped Solomon's ring onto his finger and held it out. Nothing happened.

"You look like the Green Lantern," Bones said.

"I thought you weren't into superhero movies."

"I'm not, but that movie sucks so bad I like to drink beer and mock it."

"Sounds fun, actually," Isla said. She stood, hands on hips, gazing at the blank wall. "Let me see the ring."

Maddock handed it to her and she slid it onto the fourth finger of her left hand. "You said you tapped three times?"

Maddock nodded.

Isla approached the wall, reached up, and rapped three times on the stone with the signet of the ring.

"Behold, I will cause breath to enter into you and ye shall live." She leaned forward and blew on the rock.

Maddock knew it had worked even before the door opened. Blue lights deep within the stone began to glow, forming the shape of Solomon's Seal. The outline of a door appeared, and then the entire section seemed to dissolve, leaving an arched opening wide enough to drive a truck through.

"Where did the stone go?" Isla breathed.

"Maybe it was never there," Maddock said. "Maybe it was an illusion that the ring cleared away."

"Felt pretty solid to me," she said. "Anyway, who wants to go first?" She turned and looked at Bones. "You usually like to forge ahead."

"Sure," Bones said, "send the brown dude ahead to spring the booby traps while the white people hang back."

"I didn't mean..." Isla began.

"He's kidding," Maddock said as Bones shouldered past them and into the waiting darkness. "He complains, but he lives for this stuff."

"I live for babes," Bones called over his shoulder. "Treasure hunting is just a hobby."

The entrance to the mine was a rough tunnel, the floor worn smooth, descending into the earth in a tight spiral. Several times they had to grab the sides of the passageway to keep from sliding down.

"How did they ever haul treasure up this slope?" Bones asked. "Slave labor, I guess."

"I'm sure they used slaves, but I doubt they brought it up this way. There's probably another way out. This is just the path laid out for future seekers."

"They didn't exactly roll out the red carpet for us," Bones said, ducking beneath a low spot in the ceiling. "Just a bunch of dirty, slippery rocks."

"Look in front of you." Isla aimed her flashlight straight down the tunnel.

Up ahead, the passageway leveled out and split into two. Each was guarded by a statue. The figure on the left was an ancient warrior sharpening a curved sword with a whetstone. The figure on the right was also a soldier, but this one held a pair of crossed swords.

"Which way do we go?" Isla asked.

Maddock considered the choices. He and Bones had seen things like this before. Safe passage through required a correct interpretation of subtle clues.

There was only one significant difference between the two figures that he could see—one held a whetstone in his left hand while the other held a sword. He tried to think of any connection with Solomon. And then it hit him.

"It's the passageway on the right."

"How can you be certain?" Isla eyed the statues doubtfully as if they might spring to life at any moment.

"One of Solomon's most famous proverbs. 'As iron sharpens iron so a friend sharpens a friend.'"

"That's flimsy, Maddock," Bones said.

"Got a better idea?"

The big Cherokee considered, then shook his head. "Nope, but I'm not going first this time."

"Fair enough." Keeping an eye on the statue, Maddock walked past it and into the tunnel. When he'd gone twenty paces he turned and called for the others to follow.

The passageway doubled back on itself and they soon came to another divide. There were no statues here. Only a carving of a horse above the left-hand passage, and a herd of stallions above the right.

"I got this one," Bones said immediately.

Isla frowned. "You're joking."

"The three sins of Solomon," he said.

Maddock scratched his chin. "Never heard of them."

"I grew up in the Bible Belt, where everybody's obsessed with sin and hell. Believe me, I heard all about it."

"Are you planning on filling us in?" Isla asked.

"The Bible says a king should not multiply horses, wives, or gold. Solomon did all three."

"So, the one horse, then?" She looked over at the passage on the left.

"I guess it's my turn to go first." Grinning, Bones passed beneath the horse carving. "Unfortunately for you two, I made it. Come on."

The next divide followed the same theme, with a statue of a single woman on one side, and a group of scantily clad figures on the other.

"I don't understand," Isla said, as they reached another, this one with a single coin engraved on one side and a pile of gold on the other. "Solomon was quite the sinner. He enjoyed the pleasures of the flesh, amassed women and material wealth. Why would he create this memorial to his wrongs?"

"Maybe he repented," Maddock said. "Wanted whoever followed him to be better."

"Perhaps." They chose the proper tunnel, rounded a corner, and stopped.

Isla's eyes were wide as saucers.

"I don't believe it."

Nomi paused in front of the pair of statues. They were quite similar, save for the fact that one held two swords while the other held a sword and a whetstone. Otherwise, neither passageway was marked.

"Which way?" Cleo asked.

"I don't know." She scanned the ground to see if Maddock and the others had left any tracks. Nothing but solid stone.

Ronald let out an impatient grunt. "I'll take one; you take the other." He gave Cleo a shove toward the passageway on the right while he entered the one on the left.

"Ronald..." she began. Before she could continue, the ceiling above him collapsed.

Ronald staggered back, blood streaming from a gash in his forehead. "What in the hell?" he groaned.

"Booby trap," she said. "We must proceed with caution."

"Brilliant deduction," he grunted.

Nomi ignored him. She took time to bandage his wound before they proceeded.

Hand resting on her pistol, she shone her flashlight back and forth, suddenly alert for more dangers than those posed by their quarry.

"It's magnificent," Isla gasped.

Maddock could not disagree. They stood on a wide ledge. A deep chasm lay before them, the opposite wall filled with mine shafts like a honeycomb. Everywhere they shone their lights, veins of gold sparkled beneath the beams.

Far below, Maddock could just make out ancient mining tools: pickaxes, shovels, and carts. Here and there, mounds of dross stood interspersed with smaller piles of ore.

"Gold everywhere," Bones said.

"I can't imagine how much wealth is contained here," Isla said. "Look at all those mining tunnels."

"How do we get down?" Bones asked.

Maddock turned to inspect their surroundings. He whistled when he saw what lay behind them.

"Guys, check this out."

A crescent moon-shaped cut had been scooped out from the bedrock behind them. A series of ornate columns divided the space into eleven galleries. In ten of them, Bronze Age weapons stood propped against the wall—spears and swords. At the foot of each lay a pile of bones.

"It's like they set guards here," Isla said, "and they stood here until they died and rotted away."

Maddock thought that was exactly what it looked like. Bits of armor and scraps of rough fabric lay amongst the bones.

"Do we want to hazard a guess as to who they were guarding?" Flanked by Bones and Isla, Maddock approached the gallery in the center.

The back of this gallery was adorned with Solomon's Seal, the star rendered in gold and aquamarine jewels set in the wall. But it was what lay beneath the seal that drew his interest.

Their flashlight beams shone on a marble coffin adorned with cherubim and seraphim. Inscribed on the lid were the Hebrew letters SLMN.

"Solomon," Isla breathed.

Maddock gazed at the coffin, soaking in the knowledge that he was looking at the final resting place of the famed Hebrew king. Something, he realized, didn't add up.

"Isla, why does the Sisterhood want the mines?"

"What do you mean?" she asked.

"There's a ton of gold here; I get that. But the Sisterhood already has money. And it's not like this place is filled with treasure they could just scoop up and carry away. It would have to be mined, which would involve expense and complications. It doesn't make sense to me."

Isla took a deep breath and let it out in a rush.

"I think the answer might lie inside the coffin."

"Sweet. I've been wanting to take a look," Bones said.

He and Maddock worked the heavy lid free and carefully slid it to the floor. Isla shone her flashlight into the coffin.

The mummified remains of King Solomon lay before them. Hollow eye sockets stared back at them, his teeth drawn back in a haunting rictus. Bits of dried flesh were stretched out over a skull adorned by a headdress of gold and jewels. A golden breastplate, also jewel-encrusted, lay across his chest.

"That would buy a lot of beer," Bones said.

In his left hand, Solomon clutched a copper scroll. In his right, a staff.

The staff was made of dark, polished wood. Each end was capped with iron and a brass band ringed the center. Strange symbols were carved into every inch of the surface. Maddock had just leaned in for a closer look when a voice rang out.

"Put your hands in the air slowly, or you all will die."

CHAPTER 35
Tsingy de Bemaraha, Madagascar

Maddock turned slowly, hands above his head. Had he been alone, he might have tried something different, dive behind the coffin and come up fighting, perhaps. But he was not alone and he didn't know what they faced. He knew Bones could fend for himself but not Isla. The only time she'd ever come under fire, she'd lost her composure and fled.

Triple flashlight beams shone in his direction. He could tell by their positions that they rested on the floor. No good for targeting.

"Last time we were together, I didn't make certain you were dead, Mister Maddock. I won't make that mistake again."

"Nomi."

"Did you miss me?"

"Not especially. I prefer a girl who sticks around." He had not intended that as a slight against Isla, but he could tell from the hurt expression on her face that she had taken it that way. Too bad. They had more pressing concerns at the moment.

"I intend to stick around," Nomi said, "long after you're gone."

Maddock's fingers itched to go for his pistol, but he'd never get to it in time. He could just make out the three figures arrayed before them, all down on one knee in a shooting position, weapons aimed with steady hands. Any sudden move and they were all sure to die.

"Give me the ring," Nomi said.

"I don't have it anymore."

"Lie to me again and you all die. Give it to me."

"Fine." Slowly, Maddock brought his hands down, reached into his pocket, grabbed a coin, and tossed it into the air toward Nomi.

That was the signal. As Nomi's eyes followed the arc of the shiny metal object, Maddock dove to the side, rolled, and came up with weapon in hand.

Bones had tackled Isla and was shielding her with his body as he drew his weapon and fired from a prone position.

The intruders returned fire. Maddock heard a cry of pain, but didn't know who had been hit.

Nomi stumbled backward, teetered on the edge of the chasm, but caught herself just as she snatched the coin from midair.

Maddock fired off a single shot in her direction and rolled to the side. He saw her dash away, clutching her wounded hand to her chest.

It was chaos. Flashes of gunfire. Bullets flying, ricocheting. Flashlights kicked, rolling crazily in every direction. Maddock tried to choose his targets but could not tell who was who.

"Stop!" A woman's voice, strong and terrible, boomed throughout the cavernous space.

Isla rose up from behind the coffin, Solomon's staff clutched in both hands. Red sparks danced along its surface, the symbols glowing like embers. On her left hand, Solomon's ring blazed a brilliant, icy blue that burned the eyes to look at it.

"Isla! Get down!" Maddock shouted.

Either she could not hear him or she chose to ignore him. She brandished the staff, her eyes alive with the same light as the ring.

Shots rang out from Nomi and her companions, but none of them struck Isla. Whether they missed or were deflected by some mystical power Maddock could not say. Intent on doing his part, he aimed a shot at the spot where he had seen the closest muzzle flash, then dodged to the side as someone fired back.

Isla looked to her right, then to her left. "The breath of life!" she cried. "Rise!"

Flickering trails of red light flowed out from the staff, each settling upon one of the piles of bones that guarded the remains of Solomon. At the first touch of the light, the bones began to assemble themselves, forming ten massive skeletal soldiers who hefted their weapons and marched forward.

"Kill them!" Nomi shouted. She and her companions opened fire. Bullets shattered bone, pinged off of sword blades and spear points. One skeleton went down, its knee shattered. Then another. But both continued to crawl forward.

The pace of gunfire slowed and then abated.

"Run!" One of Nomi's companions broke and ran, heading for the exit. A skeleton warrior stepped forward and swung its sword.

Maddock just had time to recognize the fleeing man as Ronald before the sword took the man in the throat, cleanly severing his head from his body.

At that, Nomi and her other companion, Maddock assumed it was the man called Cleo, turned and fled. The skeletons gave chase.

Terrified, Nomi and Cleo ran right off the ledge and plunged into the chasm below. Like lemmings, the skeletons followed behind them.

Maddock rose and turned to Isla, and gasped at what he saw.

A crimson nimbus surrounded her. Her head was thrown back, her face a mask of ecstasy. Winds began to swirl. Maddock remembered the stories of Black Caesar, how he could call up a storm to disable a ship before he captured it. Gale force winds buffeted him, driving him toward the ledge.

"Isla! Stop it!"

The winds continued unabated. Maddock leaned into them, trying to get to Isla. He suddenly realized Bones was nowhere to be seen. Where was he?

He spotted his friend, soaked in blood, crawling out from behind the coffin.

"Isla, you've got to get a grip on yourself!" Maddock shouted.

But Isla could not hear him and now he knew why. The glowing red light around her had taken on a human form—a muscular form with slanted eyes, a sharp chin, pointed ears, and fangs.

He remembered another of the Solomon legends Isla had collected. Solomon had used the ring to control the djinn, both good and evil, to do his bidding. An evil spirit had taken control of Solomon, persuaded him to hand over the ring, and that spirit had wielded the power of Solomon for forty days and nights before Solomon recovered enough of himself to wrest control from the malevolent spirit.

As Maddock looked up at the glowing red figure, he knew that he had truly seen the face of evil.

He lurched forward, the wind nearly strong enough to support his weight.

"Isla," he pleaded, "you've got to fight it."

The djinn bared its fangs and leered at him. Isla looked at him, her eyes still glowing. There was no sign of recognition there. Only malevolence.

Bones had crawled within arm's reach of her. With a grunt of pain, he made a grab for the staff. She snatched it away and cracked him on the temple with the iron tip. He fell dazed to the floor.

Maddock racked his brain, trying to remember any more details of the legend. Solomon had used the ring to control the djinn: iron to control the evil djinn, bronze for the good.

His eyes fell on the bronze band around the staff. He dropped to his knees and crawled forward, head down, like a supplicant.

"Don't hurt me," he pleaded, inching closer. "Please. I won't fight anymore." Closer…closer.

And then he leaped. One hand closed around the brass band, the other clamped down on Isla's left hand, his palm pressed against the hard surface of the ring. Would it be enough?

He felt a flicker, a sense of a faint presence there, just as he'd felt every time he'd put on the ring. He focused all his thoughts on communicating with this presence.

Help me. Save us.

A blue mist emanated from the brass band on the

staff, forming into an amorphous blue blob. Maddock concentrated harder, pouring his will into the shape until it too formed into the shape of a djinn. A single thought sent it flying into combat with the red spirit.

Maddock could tell by the faintness of his djinn that it was not here as strongly as the evil spirit, but it fought with zeal.

The djinn pummeled, clawed, bit, and tore at each other. Maddock felt as if he and Isla were inside the spirits as they battled.

Meanwhile, a similar battle was taking place between him and Isla.

He struggled to wrest the staff from her grasp, but the djinn had multiplied her strength, and it was all Maddock could do to remain on his feet. He continued to say Isla's name, to remind her who he was, who *she* was, to urge her to come back to him. From time to time, he thought he saw a flicker of recognition in her eyes. In those moments, his djinn gained the upper hand over the evil spirit. But the recognition inevitably faded away, and the red djinn regained the advantage.

Maddock's strength began to fade, and with it, his djinn. The evil spirit wrapped its long red fingers around the blue's throat and squeezed, letting out a wicked laugh.

Maddock fell to his back. Isla, still possessed by inhuman strength, pressed the staff hard against his throat.

"Die!" she hissed in a voice that was not her own.

Maddock's body began to react to the lack of oxygen. He fought with all his might, but could not overcome the demonic power that controlled her. Darkness closed in around the edge of his vision. The blue djinn flickered like a guttering candle.

Strangely, he thought of Kendra. Rather, he remembered something she had said.

"Knowing a spirit's name makes a big difference. They are compelled to respond to you, if only briefly until they can summon the strength to resist."

What was the name of the djinn that controlled Solomon?

"Sakhr," he grunted. "I call you by name and command you to obey me."

The djinn's eyes went wide with shock. It froze, its light beginning to fade. Resurgent, the blue djinn, shining brightly, struck. It drove its fist into Sakhr's chest and tore out its heart.

Sakhr threw back his head and let out a roar like a thousand hurricanes. Flame poured from his mouth, tears like molten lava rolled down his cheeks.

Maddock felt the pressure on the staff release. He shoved Isla off of him, tore the staff from her grasp, and flung it away. It clattered across the stone, its iron caps sending up red sparks, and tumbled over the ledge.

Hastily, Maddock seized Isla by the wrist and tore the ring from her hand.

The djinn vanished.

All was eerily silent.

"Maddock, what happened?" Isla whispered. "We were standing at the coffin. Someone told us to put our hands up. I remember I grabbed the staff, thinking I could use it as a weapon. And now I'm here."

"I'll tell you what happened." Bones' voice, weak yet gruff, rang out. "I got my ass shot and then you smacked me on the head with that freaking staff. I think you got blood in my hair."

Maddock left Isla where she lay and hurried over to Bones.

"Where are you hit?"

"Shoulder," he said. "Nothing critical, but damn, it hurts. Messed up my jacket, too."

As Maddock tended to Bones, he filled Isla in on all that had happened. Isla was horrified to learn what she had done.

"Well, you did save us," Maddock said. "You just got a bit out of control there at the end."

"That must be why Solomon let the mines fall into legend," Bones said.

Maddock nodded. "I'll wager he arranged for the staff and ring to be split up after his death so that Sakhr couldn't be loosed again."

"Wonder why he didn't just destroy them?" Bones asked.

"I don't know. Maybe they can't be destroyed." Maddock held up the ring. "But I think if we were to drop this thing into the deepest part of the sea, that would work just as well."

"As long as it doesn't end up in a fish's mouth," Isla said.

Maddock chuckled. "That's a chance we'll have to take. Let's get out of here."

EPILOGUE
Glasgow, Scotland

The call came from a private number but Brigid knew who it was. She had no interest in talking to Nineve any more often than absolutely necessary, but in this case, she was eager to hear from any member of the Sisterhood. She had not heard from Isla for several days and her daughter was not answering her phone or returning calls for messages. Perhaps Nineve could tell her where Isla was, or at least let her know that Isla was all right.

"I need to talk to your daughter," Nineve said the moment Brigid answered. "Where is she?"

Brigid's heart pounded out a rapid beat. "I had hoped you could tell me. I have not heard from her for some time."

"You're lying," Nineve said flatly.

"No." Brigid saw no point in pleading her case any further. Nineve would believe what she liked.

"Gowan was found dead yesterday."

Brigid frowned. "The man who was working with Isla?"

"Correct."

"But Isla was not..." Brigid could not finish the sentence.

"Isla has disappeared. A security camera spotted her near Heathrow the night she and Gowan fell out of contact with us. We're still working to find out if she did leave the country, and if so, where she went and with whom. Make no mistake, we will find out."

"I hope you do," Brigid said. "Doubtless she was running from whoever killed Gowan."

A long silence hung between them, each trying to wait out the other. Finally, Nineve went on.

"Gowan was shot from behind at close range. The bullet was the same caliber as the pistol we issued to Isla."

"That doesn't mean…"

"Listen to me," Nineve barked. "I am not a fool. The two of you have conspired in this to betray me. Mark me well—if Isla does not return to Modron and accept the consequences of her actions, it will mean war between the Sisterhood and the Tuatha de Danaan. And I will not stop until every last Tuatha is dead."

She ended the call.

Brigid stared at the screen, pondering her next move. Finally, she sat down, typed out a long text message to Isla, and hit send.

She poured herself a tall glass of Scotch whisky and sat. Now the waiting game began.

Antananarivo, Madagascar

Isla rolled over when she heard her phone vibrate. Beside her, Maddock slept soundly. She smiled at the memory of the night before. It was what she had wanted for so long. And now it was real.

She reached out and placed a delicate finger on a ragged white scar, one of the many that covered his muscular body. She found them oddly erotic, symbols of his courage and strength. He'd told her there was a story behind each one, and she couldn't wait to hear him tell the tales. There was so much about him she still didn't know.

Rolling over, she picked up her phone and unlocked it. She assumed it was another message from Nineve, or perhaps from her mother. She couldn't wait until she was safely back in the States. Maddock had promised his friend in the CIA would help her start over with a new identity. Once that had been achieved, she would find a way to let her mother know she was alive and well.

The message was from her mother, and Isla read it with an increasingly sick feeling. War between the Sisterhood and the Tuatha? How many would die? And every death could be laid at her feet. She couldn't allow that to happen.

She didn't know how long she sat there trying to think of any possible solution other than the one she was considering. She considered waking Maddock, but she was certain she knew what he would say. He'd tell her to keep out of it, that those people had made their own beds. What's more, the moment he learned what was happening would spell the end to her plan.

Tears welled in her eyes as she dressed in silence. If only there was another way. This time, he would not forgive her.

Her throat knotted as she took Solomon's ring from the pocket of the pants he'd discarded on the floor. Her hand was on the doorknob when she turned around. She couldn't leave without an explanation of some sort. She grabbed the hotel pen and paper and scribbled out a hasty note before departing. It was not until she arrived at the airport that she took out her phone and made the call she'd been avoiding.

"It's me," she said. "I can give you Solomon's Mines."

End

ABOUT THE AUTHOR

David Wood is the author of the popular action-adventure series, The Dane Maddock Adventures, and many other works. He also writes speculative fiction under his David Debord pen name. When not writing, he hosts the Wood on Words podcast. David and his family live in Santa Fe, New Mexico. Visit him online at www.davidwoodweb.com.

Made in the USA
Middletown, DE
06 August 2020

14572326R00139